The Highest House on the Mountain

The Highest House on the Mountain

MERCIER PRESS
IRISH PUBLISHER – IRISH STORY

MERCIER PRESS
Cork
www.mercierpress.ie

First published in 1961 by Progress House [Publications] Ltd.
This edition 2016

ISBN: 978 1 89817 501 8

10 9 8 7 6 5 4 3 2 1

A CIP record for this title is available from the British Library

Highest House on the Mountain is a copyright play and may not be performed without a licence. Application for a licence for amateur performances must be made in advance to the Drama League of Ireland, The Mill Theatre, Dundrum, Dublin 16. Terms for professional performances may be had from JBK Occasions, 37 William Street, Listowel, Co. Kerry.

Printed and bound in the EU.

To Michael and Joan

INTRODUCTION

Writing an introduction is as tricky as writing a reference— too many compliments sound insincere, and to be critical is surely as ill-mannered as drinking a host's whiskey and telling him you know a better brand. Still, the risk must be taken to acknowledge the compliment of having been asked by the author to introduce his play.

And so I will chance an introduction—but not about the play. I know 'The Highest House on the Mountain' too well to be dispassionate about it. I lived with it from the day I was asked to direct, through the usual first-production struggle of alteration, emendation and re-writing, until it was staged and became the longest runner of the 1960 theatre festival. Such an association is too intimate for critical detachment, and I beg leave to be excused from comment.

Instead, I would like to say a few words about the author—risky, too, perhaps, and I hope neither ill-chosen nor ill-timed.

John Keane's place in the theatre is unstable. Praise and blame for his work have been extravagant—he has been identified as a sort of deep-south-Kerry white hope, and dismissed as a Bouccicault reactionary; his plays have been called 'lyrical', 'nasty', 'powerful' and 'melodramatic'— but no one can deny that he is there [very much there] and that he is successful.

Theatrically John Keane is a man from outer space. He made his name under freak circumstances. 'Sive' caused a sensation entirely through amateur production, and 'Sharon's Grave', also successful, again was launched by amateurs. This was excellent for amateur drama, but at the time I wondered if it was the best thing for John Keane, the playwright. The reward of professional efficiency is to make good work better and inferior work good, and even an effective writer like Keane needs direction that amateurs are unlikely to provide.

I was particularly pleased to be asked to produce one of John's plays. I had adjudicated his previous plays publicly and not all my comments were complimentary—indeed on the technicalities of construction I found many flaws—but I was insistent on his best qualities as a playwright, exciting invention of character, lively dialogue, and the ability which must come from some deity of the Reeks to hold an audience and fill the house. But what effect had success had upon him? How would he adapt to professional treatment of one of his scripts?

An author is, in a way, at the mercy of everyone connected with a production. Once the script is out of his hands things can happen to it that sometimes delight and often chagrin a writer, who may wonder pettishly who was responsible for the thing in the first place. Some, I suppose, get toughened and try to console themselves with, as Coward puts it, "the fruits of commercial success". Sometimes they squeal in anguish and depart with the script in an affronted hip-pocket "but—good sense, or determination, or humility, or what-you-will prevailing—they usually turn-up again.

Producers feel that authors are in the way [no doubt a reciprocal emotion] and find it difficult to be sympathetic towards the expectant-father gibberings in the waiting room of rehearsal. An anonymous benefactress [I'm sure it was a woman] was she who first thought of sending father to buy the cigars while mother got on with the job. In the theatre the best way to occupy an author is to engage him in making out a list of complimentary seats for his friends.

When I first met John B. Keane I was impressed by the fact that he neither pretended nor thought that he knew it all. Any changes suggested for the good of the play were willingly embraced and tiresome rewriting did not irk him. He was not subdued by the take-over atmosphere of a professional presentation, but had the good sense and humility to realise that by observing the work of professionals he could improve his own.

Ideas come to a writer without effort, the hard work is in expressing these ideas selectively and cogently within the limitations of a three-act play. A too-facile flow of ideas is John Keane's greatest enemy; when he can discipline his writing by a mastery of craftsmanship his boisterous imagination will not be straightjacketed but will be more effectively expressed through conciseness.

If there is in what I have written an inference of diminishing John Keane's previous work, that is not intended. Only churlishness would make one sour his success, and I write this merely as my reaction to a writer I found gifted and hardworking, who has the qualities for successful writing and who is intensely interested in mastering the high art of the theatre.

John B. Keane has years of writing before him, and I hope that time will bring a more balanced judgement on his work. Let those who venerate him delay apotheosis for posterity, and let those who hate him not be over-anxious to push him into the Pit. In simple terms—give the man a chance.

BARRY CASSIN.

'THE HIGHEST HOUSE ON THE MOUNTAIN' was first presented by Orion Productions at the Gas Company Theatre, Dun Laoghaire, with the following cast:

Mikey Bannon	MARTIN DEMPSEY
Sonny Bannon	PAT NOLAN
Sheila Moloney	JACQUELINE RYAN
Patrick Bannon	GERRY SULLIVAN
Julie Bannon	ANNA MANAHAN
Connie Bannon	GERRY ALEXANDER
Two Countrymen	PADDY MacGOWAN
	TOM NOLAN

Production was by Barry Cassin
and Setting by Robert Heade.

ACT ONE

SCENE 1

The action takes place in the kitchen of a farmhouse in South-Western Ireland. The time is the present. It is the flight time of a day late in December. Two men occupy chairs near the fire. One is reading from a newspaper. He is sixtyish. He wears overalls, cap and hobnailed boots. He is Mikey Bannon. The other is younger, fiftyish. He wears an old suit of black material, with the coat collar pulled up and about his neck. He holds the lapels together near the throat. He is barefooted, pale and dejected of face. He is Sonny Bannon.

Mikey   Did you ever hear better than this?
[Sonny looks up]

Mikey   'Civic Guard destroyed by goat in Tipperary'. Great God! Nothin' left but the badge on his cap an' the buttons of his coat. The father o'nine children and a brother a priest. The goat was treated by four veterinary surgeons. Needles was used on him but he died as a result of eatin' the Guard. *[Lays down paper]* Great God! There's no one safe in Tipperary. If the goats are like that, what way are the donkeys and horses.
[Sonny scoffs unbelievingly]

Mikey   All right! All right! I was only makin' it up, but sure I thought it might bring a smile to your face or knock a laugh out o' you. Are you cold?

Sonny   No.

Mikey   Whist, maybe it's them. An' sure they'd hardly be here yet. Sonny, will you talk to the young couple when they come, and let on you're natural, the same us all? Will you, Sonny?

Sonny   'Tis nothing to me.

Mikey   Will you shake the girl by the hand, anyway? 'Twould put her at ease in a strange house.

Sonny   I'll do that for you, Mikey. I will. I'll do that for sure.

Mikey   Ah, sure, I knew you would … Have you the hurt bad to-night, Sonny?
[Sonny nods]

Mikey   Where have you it to-night, Sonny?

Sonny   *[Puts finger to chest]* Here! Inside here 'tis!

Mikey   'Tis better than havin' it in the head, all the same, Sonny. Anything is better than havin' it in the head. Maybe if you aren't too bad, you'll talk to the girl … *[Lifts hand before Sonny can reply]* Only the bare word. Only if she'll ask you a question. You needn't let a hum or a ha out o' you otherwise.

Sonny   Sure, I don't know what I'll do. *[Panicky]* What'll I do if she says something to me? Sure, I wouldn't know what to say. I'd only leave yourself and Patrick down.

Mikey   I know 'tis hard for you, Sonny … *[Cheerfully]* Look! Did you ever notice the way people do be when they're talkin'? One says to the other … 'Oh, hello, is that you? How's the hay by you this year?' Then the other fellow says … 'Hay? What hay? How's your own scutterin' hay?' You see, Sonny, that's what comes of these fellows who make bold with their talk. The right way is to say nothin' until this fellow opens his mouth first. Now, tonight, if the hurt isn't too bad with you, let you do the same.

Sonny   I'll try it for you, Mikey. I'll do my best anyway.

Mikey   What's that … Did you hear a step on the road? Listen! *[They both listen]*

Sonny   Someone that strayed off the main road maybe or a wanderin' dog.

Mikey   I have my doubts. If 'twas a dog you'd hear him scrapin' at the door and if 'twas a body gone astray they'd knock lookin' for direction. *[Goes to door cautiously]* Don't make a tittle and we'll see. It could be some robber stealin' hens. *[He opens door suddenly and calls out]* Who's there? Who's there, I say? Come out till I see you.

Sonny   *[Tremulously]* Who is it?

Mikey   'Tis a girl that's standin' out there!

Sonny   A girl!

Mikey   She's hidden beyond the corner of the byre. *[Calls out to the girl]* Come out girl. You'll come to no harm, I promise you. There's no one here but myself and my brother. *[Pause]*

Sonny   Is she comin'?

Mikey   *[Retreats a little into kitchen]* She's comin' all right, whoever she is.
[Sonny rises a little fearfully and seems to withdraw a pace]

Sonny   Who would she be?

Mikey   'Tis Sheila Moloney, Ned Moloney's daughter. What's she doin' wanderin' around in the night?
[Retreats further]
[Enter Sheila Moloney]

Mikey   God save you, Sheila. Is there anything the matter at home that you're out so late?

Sheila   *[Nervously, guiltily]* No ... no ... *[Notices Sonny]* Hello Sonny.

Sonny   Sheila.

Mikey   Well, will you sit up to the fire.

Sheila   No, no thank you.

Mikey   Will I walk back home a bit of the road with you so?

Sheila   No, no need. I'll be all right… *[Unconvincingly]* 'Twas how the turkeys broke out and I thought they might have strayed this way.

Mikey   Get a light, Sonny, and we'll search for 'em.

Sheil   Oh, no, no, my brothers will do that.
[Mikey and Sonny are obviously puzzled].

Sheila   I'd better get back home now. Good night to ye.

Mikey   Good night.
[Hurriedly exits]

Mikey   She wasn't lookin' for turkeys.

Sonny   *[Sitting again]* No, she wasn't.

Mikey   Would she be courtin' some fella and maybe not want her father to know? I don't like women comin' here. I'm too lonely thinkin' about them, and you know what thinkin' leads to, and God knows, I'm as human as the next man!

Sonny   She was in strange behaviour whatever.

Mikey   *[Suspicious]* She was all that *[Shuts door]* We'll drink a mug of milk now before they come. If the weather came warm now, after the Christmas, your appetite might improve. *[Pours milk and hands mug to Sonny]* Maybe the girl that's coming is a good warrant to cook. *[Goes to dresser and cuts a square of bread]* A woman is a great thing in a house, even if you never have use for her. *[Dreamily]* Man, dear, a woman that can cook is worth the winning. *[Reflects]* What would I like now if I had a cook? A roast goose now, with a good carge of pandy inside of him. Would you like a roast goose, Sonny?

[Mikey takes a mug of milk from dresser. Sonny nibbles at the bread]

Mikey   Imagine a roast goose … or chops! There's nothin' in this world or the next as sweet as a chop. Suppose now a fellow came in that door with a frying pan full o' chops, I bet you'd jump up an' eat a few.

Sonny   I wouldn't care.

Mikey   Well I'd care, I can tell you. I'd kiss the four sides of his head. There's nothin' like chops! *[Drinks his milk]* I remember to be in the village of Ballyheigue years ago when the times were bad. 'Twas a fair day. I remember to see a cattle-jobber from West Limerick eatin' chops.

Sonny   He must have been a big man.

Mikey   I tell you he was the biggest man I ever saw. From West Limerick he came. I heard afterwards that he had twenty-seven buttons in the fly of his trousers …

Sonny   Will there be a change, do you think, in Patrick?

Mikey   'Tis hardly likely. Patrick was always a quiet boy, taking after his mother, the Lord have mercy on her.

Sonny His mother was a lady.

Mikey She was all that.

Sonny I often think of her. She was a good friend to me.

Mikey I think of her myself, man. *[Lonely]* I remember not long after we married to be mowing hay in the mountain meadow. Twas a June day and I saw her comin' across the fields with the evenin' tea. My God! she was a handsome girl!

Sonny She was all that.

Mikey She sat on the mown hay and drew her knees under her like a colt an' she watchin' me eatin'. If a crumb fell to my lap she'd stretch out her neck like a swan and blow it into the palm of her hand and hold it up to my lips. She was powerful fond of me. An' do you remember her cookin'? Man, dear, she was the finest cook that ever stripped a cabbage.

Sonny Do you think we should have done a bit of decoratin' before they came?

Mikey Didn't we whitewash the front of the house and trim the hedges?

Sonny Ah, but to hang a few pictures and things and put a few flowers here and there.
[Mikey walks around and surveys the kitchen]

Mikey There's a big holy picture belong to our grand-mother in the chest below in the room.

Sonny Ah, no, 'tis too old.

Mikey A fine picture of Moses ... and two other half-starved men with whiskers—I couldn't tell you who they are.

Sonny No. It wouldn't do.

Mikey Stop!

Sonny What?

Mikey 'Tis them. That's a motor-car. You promised now, remember. *[Noise of motor car outside]* She's be new, Sonny. She won't understand.

Sonny I'll try not to leave you down, Mikey. I'll do my best.

Mikey *[Nervously]* I'll go out now an' meet them. I'll bring in their bags now. I know Patrick anyway. If she's like him, she'll be nice. I used to take Patrick fowling with me long ago.
[Exit Mikey]

[Sonny rises, goes to window, peers out and turns with a worried look. Looks, ashamedly, at his hands and feet and garb and worried about the impression he will make on Patrick and his wife. At the sound of their voices he exits hastily to his room. Enter Mikey carrying

a large suitcase, followed by his son Patrick carrying another suitcase, and a girl, Patrick's wife. Patrick wears a light mackintosh, is thirtyish, good-looking, of placid appearance. His wife, Julie, is aged about thirty, good-looking, reserved with refined features. She wears a patch over her right eye. The bags are placed on the floor. Patrick turns to his father and takes Mikey's hand in his]

Mikey Welcome home, Patrick.

Patrick It's good to see you father.

Mikey It's good to see you Patrick.

Patrick It's been a long time father.

Mikey Let me carry these bags for you … you'll be tired after that long old run from the station.

Patrick Dad, it's good to see you. There were times when my heart broke for the sight of you. And this is Julie, Dad. But for her I wouldn't be here to-night.

Mikey God bless you, girl. You'll be a good wife to him. I know by your face. *[Kindly]* Is there something the matter with your eye?
[Julie hesitates]

Patrick It's nothing, Dad, only a soreness.

Mikey Ah, 'twill mend in time. I'll bring your bags up to the room. *[Looks around]* Where did that fellow go to? *[Goes to where Sonny exited and calls]* Sonny! Sonny! Come on down here. Patrick and his missus are here. *[Explains to Julie]* He's shy opposite strangers. *[Calls again]* Come on down, Sonny. They won't say a word to you.

Patrick *[Puzzled]* Is Sonny living here now, Dad?

Mikey Ah, sure, 'twas lonesome here and he was company for me. *[To Julie]* Sit down, girl. Sonny is my brother … Patrick's uncle. He has a house of his own an' a bit o' land on top o' the mountain. *[Calls again]* Come on down, Sonny.

Patrick Dad, Dad, but sure he won't be here all the time, Dad?

Mikey Ah, sure, he'll go back to the top o' the mountain after Christmas.

Julie It's all right! Really, it is.

Mikey He's coming down, I think.
[Enter Sonny]

Mikey Come on, Sonny. 'Tis only Patrick and his wife. *[Mikey takes Sonny by the hand leads him to Julie]* This is Julie, Sonny—Patrick's wife.

Julie How are you, Sonny? Pleased to meet you!

Sonny *[Takes her hand quickly]* Welcome! Welcome, Patrick! *[He nods and smiles]*

Mikey Bring on those bags with me, Sonny. You'll be in your old room, Patrick.

Patrick   That'll be fine, dad.

[*Exit Mikey and Sonny carrying bags*]

Patrick   Well, what do you think?

Julie   I like your father and Sonny.

Patrick   I like Sonny too, but it isn't fair bringing a girl into a house with two men inside it.

Julie   I don't mind, Patrick.

Patrick   I know, but I told you there'd be no one here but Dad.

Julie   But do you think 'twill work out? 'Tis almost too much to expect. What will they think of me? They don't know anything about me. Somehow, I can't see it working out.

Patrick   Of course 'twill work out.

Julie   Amn't I supposed to have a fortune or something? I always heard a girl marrying into a farm was supposed to have a dowry.

Patrick   Not this time. Not here.

Julie   What about your brother?

Patrick   Connie? He left here after I did. My father cleared him. He was no good. There was a bad drop in him.

Mikey   Leave it down where I told you an' don't be fussin' me.
[*Mikey heard off*]

21

Julie   Here's your father coming back. Maybe I should go to the room.

Patrick   Yes, 'twould be better.

Julie   Wouldn't it be better if you told him about me?

Patrick   Oh, God, no! You don't know the old mountainy men of these parts. I'll tell him about myself. That should do.

[Enter Mikey followed by Sonny]

Mikey   The bags are up there now. You'll be wantin' to eat after the journey?

Julie   I couldn't look at a bite.

Patrick   Maybe you'd like to go to your room a while, Julie? Maybe you'd want a wash?

Mikey   There's a basin and ewer in the room. Sonny'll go for a gallon o' spring water. Are you sure you won't have even a cup of tea? The kettle's down.
[Sonny goes immediately and takes a bucket from dresser and exits]

Patrick   No thanks, Dad.

Julie   Won't he catch cold without his shoes?

Mikey   My God, girl, he didn't wear a shoe for years.

Julie   You'll excuse me then.
[She exits room]

Mikey   *[Shouts]* If everything is not right for you just give us a shout.

Patrick   Sit down, Dad. I've a lot to tell you.

Mikey   She looks a good girl.

[Mikey sits and withdraws pipe, which he proceeds to fill and light]

Patrick   You remember when I wrote to you that I was getting married and would it be all right to bring the girl here, and you wrote back and said to come on right away and how we were more than welcome?

Mikey   Why wouldn't you be, Patrick? Your father's house and none left in it but myself, until I took pity on Sonny going strange in himself up there on the mountain.

Patrick   Well, there was lot more I should have told you Dad, but to tell you the truth I was half afraid. A lot can happen in five years.

Mikey   Ah, sure, there's no need to tell anything, man. We all did foolish things in our time.

Patrick   No, Dad! Five years was too long without ever coming home for a visit, or even writing a line to ask how you were.

Mikey   I was as much to blame as you. I never wanted you to join the army. You saw the bad road your brother went. I wanted you at home here with me. 'Tis a lonely thing for a man after rearin' two sons to have no one an' he old.

Patrick I know Dad, I know but I had to join up. A lot of the lads were going and we had it in our heads — seven or eight of us.

Mikey Sure, I'm not blamin' you, Patrick. I gave myself up to thinkin' about it after, an' maybe you were right. You were a young fellow and if I was your age who knows but maybe I'd be anxious for soldierin' too. 'Tis all over now anyway an' you're here an' you have a fine young wife. We'll fall to workin' together again.

Patrick I'll work, Dad, you can be sure of that

Mikey *[Laughing]* Do you remember at all when you were about four and you used be askin' me to carry you fishin' an' shootin' with me.

Patrick I do.

Mikey 'Twill be great man, the two of us again in the bog and the meadow...

Patrick I'll do my share, Dad, but there's more to it than that.

Mikey *[A little worried]* Wisha, why do you trouble yourself. Sure, it's enough for me, man, that you're back. Sure, if you died what way would I feel? Think of that, let you.
[Patrick does, for a moment]

Patrick Well ... when we were discharged from the Army, I

24

got a bulk sum of money. I got a decent job, clerking in the office of a garage.

Mikey   A clerk in an office! You were always good at your books.

Patrick   Well, of course, they gave preference to Army lads, too. 'Twas then I got a plan into my head. I said I'd work for a year or two and come home here and maybe buy a tractor. It was just to show you, Dad, that I wanted you to think right of me. I meant well.

Mikey   Things didn't go right for you?

Patrick   That's putting it lightly. I had a right bit of money until I met this girl…

Mikey   Julie? Your wife, a nice-lookin' girl?

Patrick   No! — not Julie!

Mikey   Who so?
        [Enter Sonny with bucket of water. He stands foolishly after entering]

Mikey   Take it up to her, man!

Sonny   Will one of ye give it to her?

Mikey   *[Smiling]* Yerra, knock at the door, man, and hand it to her. She won't bite you.

Patrick   Go on, Sonny! You'll like her when you know her.

[Hesitantly Sonny approaches door and taps on it while Patrick and Mikey exchange humorous looks]

Sonny 'Tis the gallon of water!

Julie *[Opens door and accepts water]* Thank you, Sonny!

Mikey Well Son, what were you going to tell me?

Patrick Oh, nothing, Dad —

Mikey Never mind Sonny, sure isn't he my own brother and your Uncle?

Patrick I know Dad, but sometimes it's not easy ... MIKEY Tell me about her.

Patrick About Julie?

Mikey About the other one.

Patrick Her father was manager of the garage where I worked. Her name was Eleanor.

Mikey A handsome name for a girl; I can imagine what she might be like. She threw you over for another fellow?

Patrick I gave her a good time. She was fond of a drink and I drank with her. When my money was gone, she was gone.

Mikey Ah ... And then you met Julie?

Patrick No ... not for some time. When she found me I

was … I saw Eleanor again and asked her to marry me. She laughed her head off.

Mikey And you went on drinking by yourself.

Patrick How did you know?

Mikey It's not uncommon. When something like that happens a fellow he often hits the bottle.

Patrick I hit her.

Mikey I don't understand. You hit her … It's hard to blame you, she deserved it.

Patrick Not her … Julie. Her eye, you saw her eye. I had drink taken.

Mikey You struck Julie! I don't understand …

Julie *[Off]* Patrick.

Patrick Yes.

Julie *[Off]* Can I have a towel?
[There is a pause as Mikey and Patrick look at one another]

Sonny The girl wants a towel.
[He rises to get one]

Mikey *[Recovering]* Just one minute, Julie. You can see what it is not to have a woman about the place. A house is astray girl, without a woman's hand to guide it.

Sonny *[Giving Towel to Patrick]* You bring it to her.
[Patrick exits]

Mikey *[To Sonny]* You were cryin' the time you put your hands over your face.

Sonny I wasn't.

Mikey You were! I know you inside out. Was it the hurt?

Sonny No!

Mikey Was it something Patrick said?

Sonny No!

Mikey What was it? Tell me, can't you, and make it easy for yourself.

Sonny 'Twas the thought of him hittin' the girl that made me cry. No one should hit a girl.

Mikey It wasn't Patrick struck her. 'Twas the drink in him. 'Tisn't in Patrick's nature to strike anybody. What do you think of Julie? Do you like her or don't you?

Sonny She wouldn't be laughin' at you anyway, like some of them other ones.

Mikey We'll be in for good times now when she starts cookin'. 'Tis a pity I didn't mention to Patrick, when I wrote to bring a parcel o' chops with him. *[Passionately]* Japers, man, there's music in a chop. 'Tis like a band, I tell you … fat fryin' out an' hoppin' in the pan.

Sonny   I think I'll go for a walk out around.
           [Sonny goes to door and looks out]

Mikey   Stop, Sonny; is it that you're ashamed.

Sonny   Ah, sure, I wouldn't know what to be sayin' an' we all
           sittin' near the fire. 'Tis all right for you an' for them.
           I'd only be in the way.

Mikey   You needn't say anything, man, only nod and smile.
           She's a girl who wouldn't take notice o' you.

Sonny   *[Hopefully]* D'you think she'll stay?

Mikey   Of course she'll stay? Why wouldn't she? She
           wouldn't come unless she was goin' to stay.

Sonny   Maybe she'll turn sick o' the country an' go back to
           the city.

Mikey   *[Wisely]* No, she won't go back. They're glad to
           be here. We'll have good cookin' from this out.
           [Extends his belly and pats it] I'll end up my days
           with long red plucks like a rooster an' a big white
           belly like a harvest frog.
           [Voices off]

Sonny   They're comin' down. I'll come in when they're gone
           to bed.

Mikey   *[Tries to restrain him]* In the honour o' God, man,
           wouldn't you sit down an' be natural the same as us
           all.

[Exit Sonny. Mikey shakes his head resignedly. Enter Patrick and Julie wearing shade over eye. She wears a white blouse and black skirt]

Mikey   Sit here, the two of ye. *[He seats both of them]*

Patrick   Where's Sonny?

Mikey   *[To Julie]* To tell you the truth, he's a bit of ashamed of himself with strangers in the house. I've been at him all day to stay around, but he's the kind of a man who wouldn't want to be in the way.

Julie   He'll get used to me. I think I understand.

Mikey   He has a great hurt inside of him. It's eatin' the heart out o' him.

Julie   Is he sick?

Patrick   No! It's nothing like that.

Mikey   It's something is on his mind. He'll often sit here by the fire alone till the cocks are beginnin' to crow. I was often woke up by him to hear him whimperin' like a collie.

Julie   Was he like that always?

Patrick   He's like that since I was a small boy. He has a small farm of his own on top of the mountain, a fine bit of land, dry and supporting, and he keeps cattle there.

Mikey   I brought him down here when Patrick went in the army. The mountain people didn't want to let him come. They're strange people up there. Small places. Working hard. Very clannish and secure. All the young lads and ladies up there never look at me because they think I stole Sonny from them.

Julie   Was he married?

Mikey   *[Laughs]* God! … Sonny would be in dread of his life to go next or near a woman!

Julie   It's a terrible thing to see him like that. Maybe he doesn't like me?

Mikey   He likes you, an''tis very few he likes!

Julie   'Tis a shame to see him so lonely, and out in the cold without any shoes.

Mikey   I'll go out to him a while. Anyway, the two of ye will be wantin' to have a talk. *[Goes to Door]* I won't say any more how welcome ye are, except that it does my heart good to see my son home and his wife along with him. *[Is about to say more, but goes out]*
[Exit Mikey]

Julie   Your father is a kind man. I like Sonny, too. He's gentle and considerate.

Patrick   I told you everything would be all right.

Julie   *[Fervently]* Oh, I wish I could be sure!

Patrick   You can be sure, Julie.

Julie   Did you tell your father?

Patrick   Not yet. We'll tell him, the two of us, when the right time comes.

Julie   Suppose he ever finds out the truth, Patrick?

Patrick   He never will.

Julie   We could be happy here. It's so far away from everywhere.

Patrick   We *will* be happy.

Julie   *[Hopefully, seizing his hand]* Do you really think we could? Do you really think so, Patrick? Oh, 'twould be like Heaven living here after what we've been through.
[As Patrick puts his hand around her shoulders we hear rain falling]

Patrick   You're not to worry any more now. All the years that are gone are dead forever. We're making a new start and everything will turn out fine.

Julie   Oh, you're wonderful, Patrick. I don't know where I'd be without you. I wish I could make you really feel the change this is for me. It's the peace of this place. It's like as if 'twas hidden; like a grove shut away deep in green fields. Even the rain falls differently here. It's a quiet rain, full of peace and it comes like rich whispers.

Patrick   Everything will be different now. We'll be shut away here and safe and you needn't worry about past things.

Julie   Oh Patrick …

ACT ONE

SCENE TWO

[Enter Mikey in a hurry with a sack about his shoulders to Patrick and Julie]

Mikey 'Tis a terrible night outside.

Patrick Is it raining hard?
[Mikey puts the sack aside]

Mikey There's hailstones the size o' crab-apples hoppin' off the road. I pity anyone without shelter this night.

Julie Where's Sonny? Did he come back?

Mikey He's all right. He knows every bush on the road. He's shy of women. That's what wrong with him. There's no fear he'll come to harm.
[Julie rises hurriedly and goes upstairs to room]

Mikey Did I upset her?

Patrick No! ... It's just that she's so good-natured and kind to people. She couldn't bear to see anybody being hurt.

Mikey Why did she go to the room?
[Julie returns, putting on her coat. She smiles at both men]

Julie I won't be long. I'll bring Sonny in from the hail.

Mikey *[As if he would restrain her]* 'Twill cut the face from you. 'Tis no night to be out.
[Exit Julie, smiling]

Patrick *[Seeing that his father is about to follow her]* You couldn't stop her, Dad, even if you tried. She's that kind of a girl.

Mikey She's a most considerate sort of a girl to go out under hailstones. Will I go after her? She might go astray. A strange girl not knowin' a foot o' the country!

Patrick There's no need, Dad!

Mikey Was she borned in the city, Patrick? Or did she come from outside of it.

Patrick She was a country girl, Dad. She went to work in the city. She was only a little girl when she went.

Mikey *[Reassuringly to Patrick]* But, sure 'tis a wonderful girl altogether that would go searching for Sonny in the dead of night-time.

Patrick She *is* a wonderful girl, Dad, ... Dad, I want to talk to you ...

Mikey 'Tis the second time since you came you said that.

Patrick Is it?

Mikey If it's hard to say, maybe it can wait.

Patrick I must tell you now. I made up my mind to tell and I must tell you at once or not at all… I want you to know … to understand … about me … and Julie.

Mikey *[Suspiciously]* About Julie?

Patrick *[Quickly]* I mean about how I met her.
[Pause]

Mikey Go on son

Patrick *[Desperately]* People in the city are different. They don't look at life the way we do.

Mikey People are much the same everywhere, Patrick. Men and women are the same if there's enough of 'em together in the one place.

Patrick I suppose they are, Dad.
[Pause]

Mikey About the girl, Eleanor. Were you long taking with her.

Patrick About six months … One night she wanted to to go away for a week-end. I told her I had no money.

Mikey And that was the last you saw of her?

Patrick Until I asked her to marry me.

Mikey You took to the bottle then?

Patrick It was hell, Dad! Another world altogether. *[More to himself, than to Mikey]* You have to be in that world to know what it's like. Everything is different there and time goes by fast. People are different in that world, too.

Mikey How did you meet Julie?
[For the first time Mikey lifts his head and looks at Patrick]

Patrick I'll come to her. I drank what few pounds I had left and after that I drank myself out of my job. For a long time then I picked up a day's work whenever I could. What I earned I drank. I went on the bum then. One night I was knocked unconscious in a pub.

Mikey *[Angrily]* Who struck you?

Patrick I was out of my mind for a drink and I tried to steal a man's whiskey. A fellow saw me and the whole crowd in the bar beat me. They threw me out on the side of the street … *[Pause]* 'Twas there Julie found me.

Mikey What sort of a girl is she?

Patrick Julie? … The best that God ever put into the world.

Mikey After she found you … what happened?

Patrick She took me to where she lived. I don't remember much, only curious faces and passing lights.

Mikey Her people? Did they mind?

Patrick   She had no people.

Mikey   At all?.

Patrick   Only herself.

Mikey   Hm … full honours to her, to pick you from the street.

Patrick   She nursed me back to myself. She had a hard time. I used to scream at night when she'd lock me in. I used to kick the walls and smash her few pieces of furniture. One night I was distracted for the want of drink… She wouldn't give it to me … I struck her … *[Mikey sucks in his breath, audibly]*

Mikey   Oh son …

Patrick   When I looked into her hurted eyes and saw the blood on her face, I knew that in all my life I could never make up to her for that wrong. But I could try … and I have tried.
[There is silence for a moment]

Mikey   And this other one, this Eleanor, do you ever have a thought for her?

Patrick   *[Intake of breath]* Yes … I do! I can't help it. Sometimes I think it must be in all of us, the desire for a woman we can't have.

Mikey   *[Rising]* You'll find, after a while, that 'twill pass … *[Unsure of himself]* I'm sure you will, in time.

Patrick   You're a good father to me. We would have a chance nowhere but here. 'Twas the only place I could come.

Mikey   Where else would you come, in the honour o' God, only here? Only home to your own. There'll be sore need o' you on the farm. 'Tis gone to rack and ruin.

Patrick   We'll bring it back. I'll do my best, Dad. I'll work.
[Sound of door]

Patrick   Julie is coming!
[He goes and opens door]

Mikey   Don't tell me she brought him back!
[Enter Julie bringing Sonny by the hand]

Mikey   Great God! but did I ever think to see it happen!

Julie   I made him promise me two things.

Mikey   You brought him back! I'd never have believed it. What did he promise you? What were the two things?

Julie   That he would wear shoes from to-morrow forward and that he would stay indoors when the weather was bad.

Mikey   'Tis a pity you couldn't make him promise he'd go to Mass.
[At this Sonny breaks away and hurries to his room]

Mikey   There, now I made bruascar of it again!

Julie   Does he not go to Mass?

Mikey   He didn't darken the door of a chapel for the past twenty-five years. Canons an' curates came convertin' him, but he took off to the mountains at the sight of a black suit. If you brought the Holy father himself to lay a hand over him, 'twould be the same thing. Here, I'll leave the light; I'm for bed. Good night to ye.
[Exit Mikey]

Julie   Did you tell him?

Patrick   I told him about me.

Julie   And about me?

Patrick   No.

Julie   Why not. If he finds out himself, he'll never trust you again.

Patrick   He must not find out. He'd never understand

Julie   He must be told. If were ever to have peace, he must be told.

Patrick   Peace …

Julie   Peace, Patrick. Its here for us, but we must be honest, and we must not be afraid.

Patrick   Shush … *[Enter Sonny, sits on stool as Patrick goes upstairs and Julie collects scarf. Julie looks at Sonny,* *crosses back to him and puts coat on shoulders]* Ready for bed, Julie?

Julie   Goodnight Sonny.

Sonny   Goodnight, Julie.

ACT ONE

SCENE THREE

Action as before. The time is some hours later. The kitchen is dark, save for a glow where the fire is. Sonny can be seen, hunched over the fire, in his usual seat. At this time he is praying. His voice is slow, monotonous, as he says the Lord's Prayer repeatedly. Suddenly there are lights seen to penetrate the darkness of the kitchen. Also there is the noise of a motorcar. Sonny jumps up, alert. There is much commotion outside and the sound of voices—A mans and womans. There is the noise of the car departing. Then a knock at the door.

Man's Voice   *[From outside]* Open the bloody door!

Sonny   *[Advances to door]* Who is it? Who's out?

Man's Voice   It's me! It's Connie. Come on, open the bloody thing. D'you want us to perish here in the cold?

Sonny   Is there someone with you?

Connie   Never mind who's with me. Open up!

Sonny   Your father is in bed, I can't.

Connie   *[Exasperated]* Look! In the name of God, will you open the door? *[Pause—Anger]* If you don't open the bloody thing, I'll kick it in.
[Sonny hurriedly lights the kitchen lamp, then cautiously opens door]

[Enter a Man of about thirty, black-haired, stocky, jaunty. Without looking at Sonny he takes in the kitchen at a glance. He is Connie Bannon, another son of Mikey Bannon's]

Connie   Why didn't you open the door? You knew 'twas me, didn't you? You'd leave in a bloody dog before me.

Sonny   *[Awe]* What'll your father say? And Patrick and his wife?

Connie   So they're here already, are they?

Sonny   Your father'll kill you, man, when he finds out you're here. Go away while you can.

Connie   You're still a dunce at your catechism. Didn't you ever hear of the Prodigal Son? *[Turns suddenly and addresses someone outside]* Come on, Sheila and bring in my bag.
[Enter a Young Girl of about twenty]

Sonny   *[In awe—to Connie]* Poor Sheila ... why didn't you leave her along? She was only a child when you left. What do you want blackguardin' her again for? Sheila, *[Then gently]* Sheila, what happened you, girl? Did you write and tell him about Patrick coming home?

Sheila   I'm sorry, Sonny! ... You told me in confidence ... You forgot I love him.

Sonny   *[Looks at her directly]* Do you love him in earnest?

Sheila *[Hangs her head]* I do! *[To Connie who is lighting lamp]* It was Sonny who told me about Patrick and his wife coming home. He told me because he trusted me, and I let him down.

Sonny I'm sorry for you, Sheila.

Connie Still the same old Sonny. Never goes to Mass. Never wears any shoes. Lives like a hermit on top of the mountain. A bloody freak!

Sheila Leave him alone! He's done nothing to you.

Connie When did Patrick come?

Sonny He came tonight … a few hours ago.

Connie What's she like, his wife?

Sonny A nice person.

Connie You know me. Don't play games with me.

Sheila Why don't you leave him alone.

Connie Sit down and for God's sake look as maidenly as you can if my father comes in. *[Sheila sits. To Sonny]* Is he giving the place over to Patrick?

Sonny I don't know.

Connie Listen to me. I came home to get my share and I'm not leaving here without it. I've got as much claim here as Patrick has and I'm damn well going to do something about it. Now, tell me what's going on?

Sonny   'Tis nothing to me.

Connie   Isn't it? Tell me about his wife. What's she really like?

Sonny   *[Backing away]* I don't know anything about her.

Connie   You met her, didn't you? You spoke with her. You had a good look at her. You're not blind. Now, who is she.

Sonny   'Pon my soul, I don't know, Connie.

Connie   You remember the time when you wouldn't give me the money. *[Seizes Sonny by lapels … Insistently]* *[No answer]* Where's she from? *[No answer]* What does she look like? *[No answer]*

Sonny   *[Terrified]* 'Pon my soul and conscience, I don't know.
[With some disgust, Connie flings him aside, quickly Sonny exits upstairs]

Sheila   He's gone to tell your father.

Connie   He'll have to know I'm here sometime.

Sheila   Maybe you shouldn't have come!

Connie   I wouldn't be here if you hadn't told me, remember!

Sheila   I shouldn't have told you. Maybe I should have run away and come to you instead. I might have helped you more that way.

Connie Maybe you shouldn't... but I'm here! My father threw me out, but I'll pretend to be a real angel this time. I know the old man like the back o' my hand.

Sheila How much do you want? How much money do you need?

Connie I need a lot. It's a good farm ... it's maybe a bit run down. Now ... I figure I have about five hundred pounds coming to me. The main thing is to keep on the right side of the old man. *[Warning]*: You watch that! I've got to get that five hundred ... its' my last chance.

Sheila Suppose he throws you out again?

Connie Let me worry about that.

Sheila But, Connie, what about me?

Connie It's a good thing you re here. My father always liked you and your people, and he knows nothing about us.

Sheila I don't mean it like that, but what about me afterwards?

Connie *[Impatient]* How do you mean ... what about you?

Sheila Will you take me with you?

Connie *[Trying to dismiss it]* You'll be all right. I'll see to that.

Sheila *[Goes near to him]* Don't you understand? I'm no good to anybody else. I've never forgotten you. I don't care what you are or what you do to me so long as I can be with you. Don't you understand what you mean to me?

Connie For God's sakes, don't start to cry … don't do that!

Sheila You don't know what it was like for me while you were away. It's the evenings that would be my hardest time. The boys and girls were cheering and singing on their way to the dances and I would remember the times you danced with me. I'd think about you and my heart would fair break with loneliness.

Connie Ah, sure, what could I do? What do you expect from me?

Sheila How could you know what it was like for me in the long nights of winter. How would you know the emptiness of my dark lonely room and the wastefulness of my body. I called your name three full times in the dark and I asked God to send you to me to look after me from the cold and loneliness.

Connie For God's sake don't be always thinking of yourself. Have I no right to a bit of independence? I'm fond enough o' you, Sheila, all right in my own way, but Godamnit there's a limit and I can't have any woman hangin' around my neck the whole time.

Sheila I won't demand anything from you, just to be near you is all I want.

Connie   Never mind that now. If you love me as you say you do, you'll help me. If I don't get my hands on five hundred pounds in three months I'm finished.

Sheila   Was what you did in England serious? Was it very bad?

Connie   *[Urgently, hastily]* You don't say ' anything about that! I'll break your neck if you do. If I got my hands on this farm I was made. It should make at least a couple of thousand.

Sheila   But what about your father?

Connie   To hell with my father! He kicked me out, didn't he? Just because I made a silly mistake with a girl.

Sheila   *[Alert]* You didn't tell me about that!

Connie   And why should I? You were no saint, remember!

Sheila   No, I wasn't, was I? I fell for you completely. That was what you wanted. You saw to that.

Connie   Look, for Heaven's sake, when you meet my father don't give him any idea there was ever anything between us.
[Sounds of voices are heard coming from Mikey's room]

Connie   That's my father's voice. He's awake.

Sheila   He won't do anything while I'm here. Don't be afraid!

Connie   Me afraid ... afraid of an old man like that! I could break his neck. *[He edges near his father's room and listens]* He's getting out of bed. I can hear him. That blood zombie woke him. *[Goes to Sheila]*

Sheila   Will I go away and let you with him? He won't like to see me here with you. It might make things worse for you.

Connie   *[As if he could kill her]* Will you shut up and keep out of the way until I call you. *[Impatient, nervous, as if to console himself]* This is the only way to deal with him. He's straitlaced. He's a bit peculiar while there's a woman around.
[Connie backs towards fire as Mikey enters followed by Sonny. Mikey is wearing only his socks, a heavy workman's vest, and trousers. He is pulling braces over his shoulders as he enters. He stands rigidly for a moment, eyeing Connie. When he speaks his voice is charged with command and anger]

Connie   Dad ...

Mikey   Get out! Get out of my house! I hunted you from *this* kitchen years ago.

Connie   *[Pleads meekly]* But, Dad, if you'll only let me talk ... only let me explain how sorry I am ... if you'll only ...

Mikey   Go! ... Go, man, or I'll not be responsible ...
[Connie takes Sheila by the hand and brings her

forward towards his father]

Connie *[Pleads]* But, Dad … Dad, this is Sheila … Ask Sheila about me, Dad. Ask her, Dad. Go on, Dad, she'll tell you about me.

Mikey So that's why you were here earlier tonight. You, were on the look out for him. Do you want your father to turn against me! If Ned Molony knew you were here he would kill Connie, and maybe myself and Ned bitter enemies for the rest of our lives. Go home, girl, and keep out of this.

Connie Don't blame her, Dad. She can't be blamed for me.

Mikey Be quiet! *[To Sheila, not so crossly]* Did he tell you about himself, Sheila? Did he tell you about the young girl he blackguarded? Did he tell you that she's a raving lunatic behind in the Asylum, all because of him? Did he tell you about the other women? There's many a good man in these parts would kill him on sight, but for the friendship they bear me.

Sheila He was always very good to me.

Mikey He was always able to get round people when it suited him. *[Pause, then suspiciously]* What's between the two of you? *[Looks from one to the other]* Are you one of his women too?

Sheila No, you're wrong! I was in trouble about some

money I owed and I wrote to him and he sent me the money.

[Mikey looks at Connie puzzledly]

Sheila *[Quickly]* He did … he did … I could think of nobody else to turn to. He was the only friend I ever knew.

Connie That's true, Dad! I helped her. You never knew the good side of me. You never gave me a chance, Dad.

Mikey Great God Almighty! To think that you ever helped anybody.

Sheila You shouldn't be so much against him. You're his father. If anybody should help him you should.

Mikey *[To Sheila]* Is this true, girl, what he says? *[Sheila merely nods]* Did he really help you? Maybe he's only puttin' you up to it.

Sheila No! No! It's true.

Connie You could never turn me from the door, Dad?

Mikey Couldn't I?

Connie You were always fair. I've no place else to go, Dad.

Mikey You'll stay for the night and to-morrow. The day after tomorrow, I never want to see the sight of you again.

Connie Don't worry, Dad. I'll be gone.

Mikey   What hold have you over the girl?

Connie   I changed, Dad. Honest to God, you'll see.

Mikey   *[Anger]* Nothing could change you. You were born
bad—Sonny, get a candle from upstairs and we'll fix
the bed below.
[Immediately Sonny exits]

Mikey   What did you do to Sonny? He came and woke me
from my sleep and he afraid of his sacred life.

Connie   Sure, I was only jokin'!

Mikey   Only jokin'! Do you call it jokin' to frighten the wits
out of a man? I'll see to your bed.
[Exit Mikey]

Sheila   He doesn't hate you. He's just not sure of you. You
mustn't blame him.

Connie   *[Gleefully, rubbing his hands]*: Never mind … we've a
foot in. That's all that matters. We've a foot in.
*[Enter Sonny slowly down the stairs. He covertly looks
at both of them from a safe distance]*.

Connie   I'll get even with you in my own time.

Sheila   *[Insistently]*: Leave him alone! He'll tell your Dad.

Connie   He won't! *[Advances a step towards Sonny and looks
from Sonny to Sheila]* Ever hear me talk about the
time he was for Confirmation?

Sheila   I don't want to hear it.

Connie   *[Awe]* You mean you never heard the famous answer he gave the Bishop? *[Sheila turns partly away]* The Bishop asked him who crucified Our Lord. You should hear the answer he gave.

Sonny   *[Defensively]* 'Twas fellows behind me whispered it in my ear.

Connie   You know the answer he gave … *[Driving it home hard]* 'Ali Baba and the Forty Thieves', he said. *[Connie changes tone]* And you'd better say nothing to my father. Remember … I know something … *[Confidently, teasing]* I know something. You wouldn't want me to tell it, would you? 'Twould be all over the country-side in the morning. *[Mock serious]*: It might even get into the papers. All the Bishops in the country would start making inquiries. *[Sonny exits hurriedly]*

Sheila   Why do you have to bully him so much? He hasn't done anything to you.

Connie   How many more times must I tell you to mind your own business?

[Enter Mikey followed by Sonny].

Mikey   *[To Connie]* What did you do to him now?

Connie   *[Utter innocence]* Not a thing.

Mikey I know by the face of him, he's upset.

Connie I swear I did nothing. Why don't you ask him?

Mikey Well, Sonny? ... Don't be afraid to talk out.

Sonny If he said anything, tell me. *[Kindly]* Did he say anything to you?
[After a short pause, shakes his head]

Sonny No.

Mikey You're sure, Sonny?

Sonny Yes.

Mikey *[To Connie]* Go away to your room.
[Exit Connie. Sheila thinking he might wish her goodnight follows him a little way hut stops when she sees that he does not intend to turn].

Mikey What will your father think of you ... out to such a late hour?

Sheila He doesn't know I'm out. Anyway, I don't care, so long as Connie's home.

Mikey Go home, girl, and put him from your mind. He's no good to you or anyone.

Sheila Goodnight ... Goodnight, Sonny ...

Sonny Goodnight.
[Exit Sheila. Sonny sits near fire. Mikey stands, preparing his pipe]

Mikey Did you ever in all your born days see better than that and to bring that poor fooleen of a girl on top of it. He couldn't be changing for the good, could he?

[Sonny gives him a scalding look]

Mikey No, you couldn't change that fellow. But did you notice Sheila Molony … she thinks a lot of him. I have pity for the girl. What's between 'em, do you think?

Sonny I don't want to think about them. I was always fond of Sheila Molony. She's a nice girl. We'll think about something else.

Mikey Do you know what I'm thinkin' about now?

Sonny No.

Mikey I'm thinkin' about chops. The last time I ate a chop was six weeks ago and the taste of 'em is in my mouth yet. I said it before an' I'll say it again. The man that invented the carvin' o' chops should be sainted an' blessed an' a marble statue built of him an' to have him sittin' up on a black stallion with a helmet on the crown of his head.

[Sonny does not answer. Mikey looks at him closely and says gently]

Mikey Is it the hurt? *[Sonny nods]*: Is it bad by you? *[Sonny nods head]*

Sonny   It's fillin' me up to here when I look back an' think and see things now … *[Shakes head to dismiss it]* … It's nothin'.

Mike   *[Indicates room to where Connie has gone]* Was it him was the cause o' bringing it on? *[Sonny shakes his head]* Are you sure? Because, if it was, he goes … now.

Sonny   'Twill pass!

Mikey   I'll open up the settle and you can lie down an' sleep. You'll be all right. Will you be all right then, Sonny?

Sonny   I'll be all right.

Mikey   I'll put down a few sods an' we'll have a good fire. You'll be like a cow in a cock o' hay. *[Cheerfully]* 'Twill be as good as anything to sleep in front of a fire. I'll tell you about a goose I saw roasted one time an' I visitin' a house over in Causeway. There he was inside in a pan o' scaldin' gravy an' the stuffin' breakin' out through him in lumps. The woman of the house poured the gravy over him. 'Maybe', says she, 'you'll oblige us by having the dinner with us?' 'No!' says I out of politeness. 'Very well so,' she said, ''Tis wrong to force a person …'
[Enter Connie]

Mikey   What mischief are you up to now?

Connie   I came to get my bag.

Mikey That's a frightful pile o' luggage to bring all the ways from England. There isn't enough clothes in that to outfit a sparrow.

Connie I brought you something, Dad … a small present for yourself.

Mikey I want none of your presents, an' I don't want you either, after to-morrow.
[Connie, nevertheless, puts a bag on table and opens it. He looks slyly at his father and brings forth a bottle of whiskey]

Connie Look, Dad! A bottle of whiskey!

Mikey I wouldn't insult the linin' of my stomach with it.

Connie *[Proudly]* And look, Dad! *[He holds up a brown-papered parcel, only to be ignored]* Look.

Mikey *[Not impressed]* What's that?

Connie *[Slyly, proudly]* Give a guess, Dad.

Mikey *[Real anger]* Get to your room with your trash. We want nothin' from you.

Connie *[Crestfallen, but sly]* You know what it is, Dad … *[Pause]* … it's chops! … *[Significant pause]* … A few pounds o' fresh chops I bought in town to-day knowin' you liked 'em, Dad. 'Twas the very first thing I thought of, Dad.
[There is a heavy awkward silence near the fire Mikey

looks anxiously at Sonny and permits his tongue to
moisten his lips]*

Mikey *[Bitterly, helplessly, weakly—to Connie]*: Wouldn't
you go away to bed? Don't you know we're tired?
*[Connie holds up one chop for his father to see but still
Mikey does not turn his head. Sonny looks at Mikey
steadily]*

Connie I'll leave them here.
*[Connie edges towards exit, carefully watching his
father]*

Connie I bought them specially for you, Dad.
*[Connie backs slowly and exits. When he has gone
Mikey rises and circles table. Finally he pauses and lifts
chop from parcel and examines it]*

Mikey 'Twould be a holy shame to leave them so rotten.
[Looks at Sonny's back] I'll put one of these down
now for you as well.

Sonny *[Turns]* I'd never eat one of them chops. 'Twould
upset the contents of my stomach.

Mikey I'll fry a handful of em for myself ...

Sonny Surely you're not thinkin' of eatin''em now. We'll
have the first light o' day in a few hours. Can't you
wait for the breakfast.

Mikey I couldn't, Sonny. I'm only human, man.
[Mikey begins to lay the chops lovingly on the table,

feeling them with tender care. He goes to cupboard and unearths a frying pan, which he cleanses with a cloth hanging nearby. He is seen to be infinitely happy]

Sonny   The cracklin' o' the fat in the pan might wake up Patrick or Julie.

Mikey   If it woke the world, the chops are going down! *[Quickly]* I'll … I'll cover the fry with a plate. No one will hear it then.
[Sonny looks on with disapproval. Suddenly they exchange glances again]

Mikey   You're blamin' me for eatin' them. I can see it in you.

Sonny   I'm not blamin' you.

Mikey   You are!

Sonny   No, I'm not! I know you're fond of 'em.

Mikey   *[Placing chops in pan]* You're sure you won't have one?

Sonny   Not for me! Don't let me stop you, though. I don't blame you for the longin' you have.
[Mikey advances to the fire and kneels, placing pan by the fire. He then returns to cupboard with a knife and a bowl of dripping while Sonny looks into the pan. Sonny rises and goes towards middle of kitchen]

Mikey   What's wrong now?

Sonny   I'll go out.

Mikey   Are you goin' contrary altogether. You'll perish with the cold at this hour o' the mornin'!

Sonny   'Tis all equal … I'm goin' out.
[*Sonny exits, watched by Mikey holding pan in hand. Mikey shakes his head in wonder. Connie enters*]

Mikey   What do you want now?

Connie   I'd a long journey, Dad. I'd nothing to eat. I wondered…

Mikey   I offered one to Sonny. I suppose you might as well have it.

Connie   Thanks, Dad … Where's Sonny?

Mikey   He went out. Could anyone imagine him to be sane or to be holy an' watch him turn his back on a fryin' pan full o' chops. [*Shakes his head and returns to the business in hand*]

Connie   You know, Dad, it's just like old times.

ACT ONE

SCENE FOUR

Action as before. The time is shortly before noon on the following day. Julie enters with cabbage, which she places on table. She goes back to door and, looks out then returns to table and starts preparing cabbage. Enter Connie, donning his short-coat over brightly coloured shirt, from bedroom.At the sight of Julie his grumpiness changes to interest.

Connie *[Pleasantly]* What's your name?

Julie *[Extends hand]* Julie. You must be Connie. They told me this morning that you came home.
[Connie holds her hand longer than might be expected]

Connie I wouldn't have wasted all morning in bed if I knew someone like you was in the kitchen.

Julie There's some tea, if you'd like it. Dinner won't be long.

Connie No, thanks, thanks! *[Nervously]* ... Where are the others?

Julie They've gone ploughing. They've been out since early morning. Sit down. I'll get you a cup of tea.

Connie *[Looks out window, worriedly]* No ... some other time.... I'd better get down there ... I used to be the best ploughman in the parish one time. What happened to your eye?

Julie   *[Hesitates]* Oh, an accident.

Connie   Let me have a look at it. I used to be good for picking things out of eyes.

Julie   Thanks! … It's all right! … There's nothing the matter.

Connie   I was only trying to help.

Julie   Thanks.

Connie   I'd better get down to the ploughing. I see my father coming. We'll have that cup of tea some other time.
[Enter Mikey]

Connie   Morning Dad.

Mikey   Mornin'.

Connie   Did you sleep well, Dad?

Mikey   What's that to you.

Connie   I slept fine on a full stomach.
[Exit Connie]

Mikey   I see you met Connie!

Julie   Only for a minute. He was anxious to get down to the ploughing.

Mikey   Was he now? The only thing I ever see him anxious about was women or money.

Julie   Maybe he's changed?

Mikey   *[Thoughtfully]* Maybe, but I've great doubts about it. Watch out for that fellow.

Julie   How did Patrick take to the ploughing?

Mikey   Surprisin' considerin' he was so long in the city. Be God, all the same Connie was a great ploughman, I'll say that for him. Beat a fellow from Cork city in the Causeway championship. Won a medal as well, show it to you sometime. *[Turns round to survey pot on fire behind him]* I'll warrant there's something good in that pot?

Julie   A brace of pheasant Sonny brought from some fowler at the Creamery.

Mikey   You aren't jocosin' me now by any chance? 'Tis never pheasants.

Julie   *[Nods]* Two pheasant. Sonny bought them at the Creamery, plucked and cleaned them. All I had to do was stuff them.

Mikey   You worked a great change in Sonny. 'Pon my soul, but I hardly recognised him this morning with the shoes on him, with his hair combed and his face shaved. I thought he was one of them Insurance fellows; he's a new man altogether.

Julie   He's a great help to me.

Mikey *[Examines the pot again]* Did I hear you say there was stuffin' in them pheasants? *[Julie nods]* What class?

Julie *[Smiling]* Oh, just bread stuffing.

Mikey With an onion, maybe, chopped up?

Julie *[Smiling]* Maybe.

Mikey *[Rubs hands]* Onions is great for the bit o' flavour. *[Hesitantly]* I … I suppose you'll put a bit o' bacon with the cabbage to make it tasty?

Julie Yes, I might do that!

Mikey I knew there was good news in you when you walked in the door with Patrick. I didn't eat roasted pheasant in nine years.

Julie I hope you'll like them.

Mikey Like 'em! If I was for the gallows in an hour, I'd eat them. Would you believe I rode five miles on a pony that was never broke, one night after hearing there was a pig killed way up the mountain?

Julie No!

Mikey I did! That was nothin' to me. Would you believe I ate twenty-two crubeens the second mornin' of a Listowel Races, and *[before she can express surprise]* the same mornin' I done away with a plate o' strangled eggs and four big wedges o' fried liver?

Julie   You must have a terrible appetite?

Mikey   *[As if confessing]* The way 'tis with me, I never got
              enough since my wife died. I get dreams every night
              thinkin' I'm sittin'with a crowd o' fellows an' we
              havin' the carcase of a big roasted bullock in front of
              us an we all hackin' at it with knives, an' there's some
              nights I dreams I'd be on top o' the mountain alone
              with a roast leg o' mutton all to myself an' then a
              nightmare would come an' an' oul hardy warrior of a
              fox would steal up an' disappear with my leg o' mut-
              ton.

Julie   I used to be a good cook a few years ago. 'Twill be
              good to have somebody to cook for again.

Mikey   I knew from your appearance the first time I saw
              you that you were no joke with a fryin'-pan.
              *[Enter Sonny, looking greatly changed from the
              previous scene, wearing shoes, shaved and with his hair
              combed]*

Sonny   *[Shyly]* The praties, Julie.

Julie   Oh, good, Sonny. You can put them on the table. I'll
              wash them in a minute.

Sonny   *[Shyly]* There's no need. I washed them spotless in
              the water-trough. They were muddy from the pit.

Julie   You shouldn't have done that! That's a job for the
              woman of the house.

Sonny   I had nothing to do. 'Twas no trouble. Mikey, 'tis raining heavy. They won't get through with much of the ploughin'.

Mikey   *[Goes and looks out window]* By gor', there's the big white sheets o' rain rollin' down the hill like the sails o' ships. The two below ploughin' will be drowned.

Sonny   I'll go down an' call them up to the house.

Mikey   Stay as you are, an' I'll have a look at the ploughin'. One thing about Connie, he could plough a furrow as straight as the path of a spit. I'd like to spy on him makin' a furrow again, I'll bring these down to the lads.
[Exit Mikey. Sonny goes and stares into fire. Julie looks at him for a while]

Julie   I'd have been lost without you, Sonny. I wouldn't know where a thing was. With you here, it's like having an old friend.

Sonny   *[Simply]* I'll be a friend to you … Did you meet Connie? I saw him going down to Patrick.

Julie   I met him. Just for a little while. Is he married?

Sonny   No, he's not.

Julie   Why did you never marry, Sonny?

Sonny   Who'd have me? Sure no one would bother about the likes o' me.

Julie   Oh, you mustn't say that! Plenty would have you.

Sonny   *[Quickly]* Oh, no … no! … I couldn't marry! I'm not fit to marry anyone.

Julie   What's troubling you, Sonny? *[She ceases work and looks at him steadfastly]* You can tell me. Sometimes it's good to tell somebody.

Sonny   I never told anyone … I couldn't tell anyone, least of all a person like you.

Julie   Nobody is that good, Sonny. Won't you tell me? It won't shock me, and 'twill do you good to tell.

Sonny   I… I… couldn't.
[Julie goes around to where he sits and puts a hand on his shoulder]

Julie   *[Gently]* Tell me, Sonny …

Sonny   You'll only hate me for tellin'. You're the first friend I ever had, and I'll lose you by tellin' it.

Julie   I wouldn't be much of a friend if I didn't hear your troubles … and understand … tell me …

Sonny   *[Hesitantly at first]* When I left here twenty years ago I was lonesome. I have my own small way up in the mountains but it's a lonely spot. I went to the city and I got a job in the buildin' of houses. I was lonelier than ever there. Often I'd be walkin' the street and I'd hear my name called— "Sonny!

Sonny!" —and my heart was fit to burst thinkin'
maybe 'twas someone that knew me. But when Id
look around I'd find 'twas some other Sonny altogether. I could make friends with no one. This night
... no ... I can't go on with it ...

[Sonny buries his head in his hands again and shakes
his head]

Julie   [Gently] Please, Sonny, for your own sake. No matter what you tell me it won't make any difference to
our friendship.

Sonny   [Lifts head again] This night, I was workin' late.
I went to the bus stop to wait for my 'bus. There
was a woman standing there, waitin' too. She was a
goodlookin' woman. She smiled at me. The 'bus was
a good few minutes off. I don't know what made
me do it ... I don't know in the name o' God what
made me do it. I'd never in all my life even thought
like that about a woman ... I went near to her and
she looked at me as if she thought I might say
'good-night', or 'What time is the 'bus' and then I
...

Julie   God pity you, Sonny. I know how a man feels with
loneliness.

Sonny   And she screamed and she screamed, and then she
ran away and I stood there shamed for then and
forever of the thing I had in mind to do ... and then

there were men shouting and I ran from that end of the city to the other, and the more people stared at me the more I ran. I hid in a place for three days and one night I came out. I was perished with the cold and starved with the hunger. In the finish I got back to the mountain by beggin's the road home.
[He buries his head in his hands again]

Julie   The woman came to no harm, that's all the matters. She shouldn't have smiled at you.

Sonny   I never had a moment's peace these past years back thinking about her. Now you know why I could never ask a woman to marry me. With such shame upon me how could I raise my head to the level of a pure woman?

Julie   Love is what matters, Sonny.

Sonny   You're trying to make it easy for me, Julie. The world knows a sin like that cannot be forgotten. A girl like you would know it best of all.

Julie   Maybe I do know it best of all.
[Suddenly their attention is drawn, to the entry of Sheila Maloney. She stands framed in the doorway looking doubtfully at Sonny and Julie. When he notices her Sonny jumps to his feet and is solicitude itself when he approaches her]

Sonny   Come in, Sheila. Julie, this is Sheila Maloney, a neighbour of ours. This is Julie, Sheila. Patrick's wife.

[The women nod at each other. Julie returns to her work at the table. Sonny steers Sheila to a seat near the fire and stands aside, not knowing what to do]

Sonny   My father knows I was with Connie last night.
[She is agitated and somewhat unnerved]

Sonny   What did he say?

Sheila   He beat me.
[Julie unobtrusively finds out dresser and prepares a cup of tea for Sheila]

Sonny   He shouldn't have beaten you.

Sheila   *[Suddenly sits upright]* Where is Connie? They'll kill him some night. Oh, my God! … my brothers … I heard them boasting what they'd do to him. There's a whole crowd and they have it planned to get him some night.

Julie   Tell us about it.
[Sheila hastily takes cup between hands and gulps most of it down]

Sheila   They don't know I'm here; if they did they'd kill me. Some night soon they're going to watch him and when he leaves the house they'll catch him. 'Tis all planned. *[Shrilly]* You know what they'll do, Sonny … you know what they'll do to him.
[Julie takes cup]

Sonny   Now, Sheila …

Sheila   They'll cut him; they did it before to a man that got a girl into trouble on the mountain. They'll do it to Connie, too. I know they will. *[Rises]* Somebody must tell him. Somebody has to tell him.

Sonny   He'll be goin' tomorrow, Sheila. Mikey said it.

Sheila   He won't. He's going to stay.

Sonny   He's not worryin' about you, Sheila. You know the kind he is?

Sheila   I know … *[Near to tears]*… I know … but I love him and nothing else matters to me but him. You'll tell him Sonny. Promise me you will.

Sonny   All right, Sheila.

Sheila   I'll have to go now. They'll miss me … Promise me!

Sonny   I'll tell him for sure, Sheila. Don't worry.

Sheila   *[Frightened]* Tell him to leave at once. Tell him to write to me and I'll join him when I get the chance. *[Exit Sheila]*

Sonny   'Twas she wrote and told him about ye comin' here. That fellow will be the ruin of her. He ruined any woman he ever had anythin' to do with.

Julie   As bad as that?

Sonny   Ah, 'twas no trouble to Connie to be bad. He used to beat me for money and threaten me. He knows

about me and the woman. You'll hear him teasin'
me with it in time. Before he left the house he was
always at it.

Julie   How did he find out?

Sonny   One night I let somethin' slip. Mikey was away at
the time and Connie beat me until I told him all.
That's Connie, always—he wants to have a hold
over people because he's afraid to trust them. Watch
out for him. Not that there's anything he could
know about to harm you.

Julie   You couldn't believe anything bad about someone
you liked, could you, Sonny?

Sonny   Not about you, Julie.

Julie   *[Kindly]* You have nothing to be ashamed of any
more.

Sonny   How could an innocent girl like you hear these
things and not turn from me?

Julie   We're friends, Sonny; friends try to understand and
help one another. You must not think too much of
me, Sonny.

*[Enter Patrick and Connie, hurriedly, heads wet,
clothes soaked]*

Patrick   We're drenched!

Connie   'Tis a terrible downpour.

[Julie immediately finds a towel and hands it to Patrick]

Julie   Dry your hair. You'll catch your death!
[She hands Connie another towel]

Connie   I'll have to change out of these clothes. The bother is, I have nothing to change into. *[Looks hopefully at Patrick]* I didn't bring a spare.

Patrick   I have a spare suit. I hope it fits you.
[Patrick exits]

Connie   I'll collect it in your room. Won't be a minute.
[Connie exits to his own room]

Sonny   I wonder did they untackle the horses? *[He rises]*
[Connie emerges from his own room again. He is seen to be carrying something under his coat. He hurries after Patrick. Sonny looks after Connie's exit, worriedly, then looks at Julie who is busy putting cabbage in a saucepan. He calls after Connie. Enter Connie. Sonny looks at him to see if he has anything concealed but there is no evidence now]

Connie   *[Testily]* What do you want? *[Looks askance at Julie with pleasant face]*

Sonny   Sheila Maloney was here!

Connie   *[Matter of fact]* Was she? What's that to me?

Sonny   She told me to give you a message.

73

Connie *[Anxious to change]* Well?

Sonny She said to tell you to leave here now; that there was a crowd o' lads after you. She said for you to write to her an' she'll follow you over to England.

Connie What the hell? She's telling me to get out now and it was she who brought me here with her bloody letter. Like all women, doesn't know when her mind is made up.
[Exit Connie to Patrick's room]

Sonny The man has no conscience at all.

Julie I don't understand him! Patrick is so gentle and kind and then you and Patrick's father, you're so different from him.

Sonny Mikey is the strongest of all of us but he's weak too with no woman here in the house since his wife died.

Julie What was she like, Patrick's mother?

Sonny She was a pleasure to talk to and a wonder to see. Mikey was out of his livin' mind about her. I see him do things and heard him say things since that he's never say if she was alive.

Julie I don't understand.

Sonny Mikey has his failings. You'll never hear him talk of anything but food since she died. 'Tis a wonder to me he hasn't fallen in worse ways. I understand him. I know he isn't all he cracks up to be but he's a good man, a great man, to hold on the way he has without a woman. You see he's a man that's not himself without a woman to look after him.

Julie   Why didn't he marry again?

Sonny   He could have taken women time out o' mind, good marriageable women, but he was lost a bit when she passed away.

Julie   You worry about him, don't you?

Sonny   He's my brother. He was always fond of me. I know him better than anyone knows him. He needs a woman most than any man I know, but he's upright and he's honest ... *[Worried]* ... I don't know ... he might have been better off to marry again. All this talk about eatin' is only a touch-up for the loss of his wife.
[Enter Connie dressed in Patrick's clothes. He does not wear coat. He regards both Julie and Sonny shrewdly]

Connie   *[Suddenly, threateningly, to Sonny]* Didn't you untackle the horses yet?

Sonny   *[Panic-stricken]* Great God! I forgot about the horses; here' was I talkin' and the horses drowned outside.
[Sonny exits hurriedly. Connie sniggers after him]

Connie   The conversation must have been interesting. What was he doing? Telling you his life story?

Julie   The conversation was interesting. He's an interesting person and most helpful.

Connie   Are ye long married?

Julie   Not long ... just a few weeks.

Connie   Find this place dull after the city?

Julie   No, I like it. I was born in the country. I like it very much.

Connie   The nearest town is nine miles. There's a sort of village at the crossroads four miles away, two public-houses, a Post Office and a creamery. The novelty will wear off after a while. It's bound to get on your nerves sooner or later.

Julie   I think I can stand it.

Connie   What sort of work did you do in the city?

Julie   *[A little flustered]* Oh ... all kinds. You know how it is.

Connie   *[Inquisitorial role]* Any particular kind?

Julie   Well, mostly hotel work.

Connie   Receptionist?

Julie   *[A little defensively]* No, waitress.

Connie A good job if you're in the right hotel. Good tips I believe.

Julie Not bad.

Connie *[Changes tone a shade]* Ever been on the ...

Julie *[On guard]* What?

Connie You tell me 'What'?

Julie *[Heatedly]* I don't know what you mean!

Connie Where did you meet Patrick?

Julie In the city.

Connie How did it happen?

Julie *[Wholly unconvincing]* I ... I can't remember now ... At a dance I think ...or it might have been a party. Maybe it was an introduction. You know how it is?

Connie *[Suddenly]* Was he very drunk?

Julie *[Searches for time before answering]* Drunk?

Connie Drunk! I asked if he was very drunk? You're his wife. You should know.

Julie *[Realising that Connie knows, asks quickly]* Where is he? Where's Patrick?

Connie *[Reassuringly]* In his room ... There aren't any pubs within four miles. Remember, I told you ...

Julie   [*Realising she has slipped*] Oh, he's in his room. I forgot.

Connie   He's in his room all right. [*Moves towards window and looks out*] That's what I remember most about this place, is the bloody rain. Patrick will be all right. Nobody will know.

Julie   [*Advances*] Wha? ... What do you mean?

Connie   He didn't fool me!

Julie   I don't understand.

Connie   You think I didn't know what he was the minute I set eyes on him ... One look was enough ... Everybody knows what a dipso is. He'll pretend he's serious. He'll pretend he loves you just as long as you're weak enough to give him a drink—and hell stop at nothing to get it.

Julie   [*Coldly*] Go on!

Connie   The little shake in the hand. The way his face twitches sometimes ... and all his strength is gone. He couldn't plough if his life depended on it. [*Loudly, angrily, defensively*] A bloody dipso would put his mother on the street for a drink !

Julie   What did you do to him?

Connie   It wasn't what I did to him. It's what he's doing to himself.
[*Julie, frightened and shocked, advances towards him*]

Julie	Did you give him drink? Did you? *[Angrily]* You gave him whiskey?
Connie	*[Vehemently]* I didn't give it to him. He snapped the bottle from my hands.
Julie	You took the whiskey to his room? You took it to his room and you knew about him.
Connie	I took the whiskey to his room because I wanted it myself.
Julie	*[Quite broken now]* He had a chance before you came.

[Connie shrugs indifferently as Julie goes to Patrick's room. Patrick emerges, drunkenly, as she is about to enter]

Julie	Oh, Patrick, why did you do it? You promised me! *[She tries to take his arm but, drunkenly, he shrugs her off]* Patrick listen to me … Please, Patrick … *[But Patrick, drunk now does not heed her]*
Patrick	*[Drunkenly, vaguely]* Eleanor … Eleanor … *[Then loudly, with hopelessness]* Eleanor!
Julie	Patrick!
Patrick	*[Ignoring Connie—tone of regretful fixation, inevitable regret]* I'm sorry, Julie. You don't deserve it from me. *[Slumps into a chair]* *[Exit Connie]*

Patrick   I see what I've done now, Julie, but I know I can get over it. I'm certain I can. *[Drunkenly again]* I'll take so much drink every day and I'll cut it down in the end to nothing. It's quite simple. You start off by taking so many. Then every day *[Illustrates with his hands]* you reduce the number of drinks by one. Oh … Oh … I can do it easily.

Julie   *[Calmly]* Stop it, Patrick … stop it! I can't take any more of it'.

Patrick   *[Paws his face with his hands]* I'm sorry, Julie … I'm really sorry. I promise I'll never do it again.

Julie   *[Screams, suddenly, violently]* Stop it! … Stop it! … Stop it! … *[Pause—then more vehemently, in a lower key]* Stop it, Patrick! Don't do that to me any more!

Patrick   But I am sorry, Julie … and I'm going to stop.

Julie   *[Breaks down]* Leave me alone. You were supposed to help me … remember? I can't go on carrying you … I need help too.

Patrick   You never had much trouble before getting men to keep you.
[Exit Patrick. Enter Sonny. He stands embarrassed after closing door behind him. He is caught in an awkward position, not knowing what to say, yet sensing it all]

Sonny   Connie is gone off ploughin' again in the rain. No horse could get foot under rain like that but I'll bet anythin' them furrows'll be straight. I seen Patrick.

Julie Oh, Sonny !

Sonny Will I follow him?

Julie *[Vacantly]* Where did he go?

Sonny *[Opens door and permits his eyes to locate Patrick]* Towards the crossroads.

Julie He has money. *[Rises]* Are you sure he's not gone towards the ploughing?

Sonny *[Shakes head]* I'll go after him, Julie.

Julie No! I'll go!
[Julie enters her room, while Sonny stands perplexed and worried. Re-enter Julie in coat]

Sonny *[Nods]* If it's very late I'll be on the road on the look-out for ye. *[Shy, worried]* I'll be on the road the whole time in case ye want me.
[Sonny goes to window and looks after her. A very worried Sonny sits on chair. Suddenly he rises, startled. Enter Mikey]

Mikey Great God! He's blind drunk ... staggerin' away to town. He didn't know who I was when I spoke to him ...
[Julie exits]

Sonny Why didn't you follow him when you saw the way

he was? There was no one better entitled to.

Mikey   [*Advances and looks at fire*] Will she be back in time? What about the dinner?

Sonny   That's all you ever think of.
[*Mikey harrumphs doubtfully*]

Mikey   I can't send the other fellow away now if Patrick is gone drinkin' … too much work to be done. [*Nods to himself, then to Sonny*] By Gor, he can plough! An' he knows how to handle a pair o' horses. He can work better 'n two men, Sonny.

Sonny   He's no good. 'Twas him gave Patrick the whiskey.

Mikey   Patrick didn't have to take it. He's a grown man.

Sonny   I'm goin' back to my own house!

Mikey   You'll perish up there!

Sonny   I won't perish. The mountain women have the house aired and the bed is always clean for me. If I want to go, I'll go, before the Christmas is over. I'm sick of this place.

Mikey   Don't say that. You know there's no need for you to *go*, man. Is it the hurt? Is it the hurt, Sonny?
[*Edges towards the pot with air of obvious insincerity*]

Sonny   The hurt is gone! The hurt left me the minute Julie walked into the house.

Mikey What reason have you so? You must have some reason?

Sonny You know why so.
[Mikey makes as if to restrain Sonny but looks instead at pot. Then Mikey goes and kneels before fire, lifts cover from pot, sniffs and rubs hands delightedly preparatory to sampling contents. Sonny watches him from doorway]

Mikey Sonny! You're blamin' me! I can see by you. *[Looks at pot again]*

Sonny You never think of other people, always yourself.

Mikey I think of the people who are close to me. I think of *you*, Sonny, and of my two sons. I've never forgotten one of you. Look, Connie's medal for the ploughin', I had it in my room all these years, and I put it in my' pocket to remind me that I've at least one Son who is a man.

Sonny You wouldn't be thinkin'…

Mikey Am I to go to my grave and let all the years I put into this land be squandered by a drunkard.

Sonny That young girl had bad luck in her choice. No one with a single thought for her.
[They look at one another and exit]

ACT TWO

SCENE ONE

Action takes place as before. The time is Christmas Eve. It is approaching Midnight.Mikey Bannon sits at the table with Connie. Connie, having finished his meal, is smoking. He seems more comfortable in the presence of his father than previously. Julie stands at the open doorway looking out. Mikey gives her a covert glance, watched cautiously by Connie. Julie closes door quietly and enters her room without looking at either one of the men. Mikey casts an uneasy glance after her.

Connie   *[Looks at watch on mantel]* 'Twill be Christmas Day in half an hour.

Mikey   *[Producing pipe and lighting same]* A fine Christmas! Did you see if she put 'pandy' into the goose?

Connie   Oh, she did, Dad. I saw her mashing the potatoes this evening.

Mikey   He was a good goose. I picked him out myself.

Connie   God he was a great Goose, Dad. You're a great judge.

Mikey   Fifteen pounds if he was an ounce. I picked him out of an ass rail of ganders—a pampered-lookin' bla'guard with the fat dancin' on him.

Connie   'Twas good of you, Dad, to let me stay on.

Mikey   In the name o' Moses, how could I let you go with Patrick the way he is. Gallivantin' to the cross-roads or the town every day with his tongue hangin' out for booze.

Connie   There's nothing in his head now but drink, and where's he getting the money, Dad? That's what puzzles me.

Mikey   All the hens are gone, aren't they? He has them all sold. Any money I had lyin' around the house is gone. *[Indicates Julie's room]* She isn't herself since he started.

Connie   I often wonder about her!

Mikey   *[Alert]* What do you mean?

Connie   Oh, I don't know!

Mikey   *[Irritably]* What are you hintin' at?

Connie   *[Quickly]* Nothing, Dad! Nothing! Just that she's different.

Mikey   Of course she's different. She's from the city, isn't she?

Connie   *[Quickly]* That's right, Dad. That's right.

Mikey   An' she's a bloody good cook, the best I ever came across in all my born days.
[At this moment Julie, coat on, comes from her room. Connie, who senses her, touches his fathers hand slyly.

There is silence, while Julie, depressed goes to door, opens it and looks out into the darkness. There is no sound outside save the faint lowing of a cow. Julie exits.]

Connie   Like some more tea, Dad?

Mikey   No—no! If I put another thing in my belly I'd burst. There's a great content in me these days with the good dinners and the regular cookin'!
[Mikey rises and draws his chair near the fire]

Mikey   Did you hear the red cow lowin' there when the door was open?

Connie   All the cows will be calving shortly. There'll be work feeding them.

Mikey   Arra, cows calve!

Connie   *[Taking a long pull]* If Patrick doesn't stop, you'll have to hire a man … and you could have me for next to nothing and you wouldn't get any man to do the work I do.

Mikey   Hah!

Connie   I wouldn't want any pay, only a few bob and my keep. You know yourself there's a sight of work to be done.

Mikey   We'll see! We'll see! I'm for early Mass in the mornin'. You'll see to the red cow. She isn't far from her time.

Connie   Oh, don't worry, Dad, She'll be in good hands.
I'll stay up all night.

Mikey   She'll be troublesome. Call me if you can't manage
her. *[He yawns and walks towards his room]* Keep
an eye down the road for Patrick. He'll be drunk, I
suppose.

Connie   I'll keep a lookout for him. Good-night, Dad.
*[Exit Mikey. Connie paces the kitchen meditatively.
Then Julie enters again. Again she opens door and looks
out. Connie withdraws to fireplace and surveys her
shrewdly. Dejectedly Julie shuts door and is about to
return to her room.]*

Connie   Were you looking for somebody?

Julie   Never mind!

Connie   I could be useful.

Julie   *[Calmly]* Could you? Well, be useful somewhere
else. I can manage without you.

Connie   He's in town!

Julie   I know where he is. You don't have to tell me

Connie   Just trying to be helpful.

Julie   You started him off. That was how helpful you were!

Connie   Look, don't try to blame me. He'd get the whiskey
somewhere. It was only a matter of time.

Julie   I had him cured almost.

Connie   He's not worth worrying over. No man is worth that much worry, especially somebody like Patrick.

Julie   He's my husband. What do you expect me to do? Forget about him overnight.?

Connie   That should be no novelty to you!

Julie   Just exactly what does that mean?

Connie   You know what I mean!

Julie   *[Stern]* No, I don't! Suppose you tell me?

Connie   There's no need, since we both know.

Julie   Stop the hinting and come to the point.

Connie   All right if you want it straight, I'll tell you … you were on the street when you met Patrick.

Julie   *[Clutches her throat]* What do you mean?

Connie   What I said! That's what I mean! The first time I saw you I knew you were on the game. Don't try to fool me. I've known dozens like you. I didn't spend my time in London for nothing.

Julie   *[Brokenly]* I'm sure you didn't!

Connie   No, I didn't, It's always the same, isn't it? … Find some poor fool who doesn't suspect and marry him. The old story of the innocent yokel and the smart city lass.

Julie *[Growing angry]* Patrick knew. I told him. It made no difference to him.

Connie Nothing makes any difference to a dipso.

Julie God, is there anything you don't know?

Connie I knew you anyway. Knew you after one look, *[Tone of plausibility]* I'm no saint. I'm not blaming you but don't try to fool me because I could tell after the first look.

Julie *[In real anger]* And what if you did? I don't care. I gave all that up when I met Patrick. It wasn't hard to give up. Do you think it's something to be ashamed of? It was hell, that's what it was, and I've been through it. I hated every hour and minute of it. Can you imagine what it was like? Do you want the filthy details? *[Passionately, near to tears]* Do you know what a soul is—a human soul? Do you know what a lost world I was in? I don't remember when it began and I don't want to. I lived through it. *[Triumphant]* It's over now and no matter what happens it's dead and done with for ever.

Connie *[Unabashed]* That's what you say!

Julie No, it wasn't I who said it. It was someone else. He said something about a person without sin throwing the first stone. You know, it's the easiest thing in the world for a woman, any woman, to be what I was. God, it's so easy. It makes you smirk at the simplicity of it when it's done. It's easy, too, to get married to somebody with plenty of money, somebody fat and old who can't marry into his own class. They'll have girls like the girl I was when I was younger. *[Passion]* But which is worse? Which is worse tell me? That—or a dishonest marriage to someone you'll hate the sight of all your life. I was never on the streets.

Connie   Oh, high-class!

Julie   God, I knew some decent men. They were men … not like you. I know what life might have been like. I was nearly lost. *[Regains control]* Then I met Patrick and we needed each other. We needed each other. It was all right until you came. *[Hate]* You wrecked it because you couldn't understand. *[Moves chairs to table]* When are you going?

Connie   How's that?

Julie   When are you leaving?

Connie   Not for some time. With Patrick the way he is, I can't very well go. *[Confidently]* The place can't do without me now. My father knows that.

Julie   *[Turning from him]* Yes, with Patrick the way he is. *[Connie advances a step or two nearer her]*

Connie   He's not worth all the worry. I don't know why you
dislike me so much. Things could be a lot different
if we were friends.

*[Julie does not turn or move in any way.
Encouraged, Connie goes on]*

I can keep a secret. *[Advances a step nearer]* I'm not
so bad if you got to know me … It's just that I never
met a woman to understand me. I'd be good to you.
[Advances to her] I haven't stopped thinking about
you since I saw you first. What good is a dipso to
any woman? *[Puts his hands about her]*

*[Julie suddenly spins about and strikes him. Then backs
to stairs]*

Julie   Keep away from me! … Don't ever come near me
again! … I'm warning you! Keep away from me!

Connie   *[Unabashed]* Shush! You'll have everybody in here if
you don't stop. *[Smiles]* Don't play hard to get with
me. Remember … I know what you are!

Julie   And I know what you are, don't ever come near me
again!

Connie   *[Angrily]* Now, take it easy! Don't start the goody-
goody act with me. *[Advances a step]* What do you
think my father would say when I tell him?

Julie   You wouldn't dare!

Connie   Wouldn't I? Don't play around with me or you'll be
sorry.

[Connie advances towards her menacingly. Julie is about to reply when Sonny enters. Sonny looks from one to the other doubtfully and advances a pace nearer Julie. He looks fearfully at Connie]

Connie What are you staring at? … Answer me when I talk to you amadan.

Sonny I'm not looking at anything.

Connie Bah! *[As if he would strike him]* What a pimp he'd make!
[Connie exits in disgust, banging door noisily]

Julie *[Anxiously]* Well?
[By way of answer, Sonny shakes his head dejectedly, then looks at Julie despondently]

Julie Did you try everywhere?

Sonny I went through every public house in town … no sign of him in any one of them, and no sign of the bicycle.

Julie He's gone since morning. Where could he be?

Sonny He might have got drunk and gone into some house along the road or he might know I'd be searching for him and have avoided me.

Julie I hope so.

Sonny What'll we do now?

Julie   You go to bed. I'll wait up for him.

Sonny   No, I'll wait up, too. I'll go back the road again; after a while.

Julie   There was no light on the bicycle. Oh, God! What can be keeping him?
[Enter Mikey in trousers and shirt and without shoes]

Mikey   *[Sleepily]* I was asleep an' I woke up. *[He notices distress of Sonny and Julie]* Is it for Patrick you're waitin' up … No sign of him yet.

Sonny   No.

Mikey   A nice turn-out the night before Christmas.

Sonny   You'll sleep when you go back to bed.

Mikey   *[Grumbling]* 'Twas gallin' to be woke up out of it and I was just after going to sleep too.
[Exit Mikey]

Sonny   Don't take any notice of him.

Julie   I'm not thinking of him. I'm thinking of Patrick.

Sonny   Why do you worry yourself? Sure, a man with drink taken never comes to harm.

Julie   *[Doubtfully]* I wish I could believe it.

Sonny   'Tis true! Sure, God never condemned a drunkard. Didn't he change water to wine when they were all drunk at Cana.

Julie   We'll have a cup of tea.

[Julie goes and arranges fire]

Sonny   *[Chiming Bells]* There's the bell for midnight Mass. 'Tis Christmas mornin' now.

Julie   We'll have a cup of tea and you can walk back the road with me after. We might meet him.

[Footsteps outside, Julie makes for door but is stopped by Sonny. A loud knocking is heard upon the door. Julie and Sonny exchange nervous glances. Knocking persists. Slowly Sonny opens door, peers out. He speaks from doorway to some people outside. Julie grows apprehensive. The conversation between Sonny ana people outside door continues.]

Sonny   Who is it?

Second Countryman *[Off]* 'Tis the young fellow. We found him on the road.

Julie   *[Advances timorously]* Wha … What is it, Sonny? … Who's there?

[Sonny turns briefly to look at her with consternation in his face and immediately tries, by gesture, to decrease the volume of conversation without. Very worried, he tried to look unconcerned in Julie's eyes and endeavours to quiet people at door. Finally, he turns to Julie]

Sonny   It's Patrick!

Julie   *[Staggered]* … Patrick? … What's wrong?

Sonny   *[Returning from door, placatingly as he can]* Now, don't kill yourself with worry …

Julie   *[Desperate, urgent, shakes Sonny]* What's wrong with him? Where is he?
[A polite, poorly dressed, labouring type of countryman enters, sympathetic of face, wearing a hat. Looking at Julie apologetically, he takes off his hat]

Sonny   He fell from the bike back the road a bit. *[Hastily]* He just fell from the bike an' the two men found him on the road. Bring him in boys, there put him on the settle. *[To Julie]* These are mountainy lads, Julie … good friends … they have Patrick with them.
[The Countryman hurries to doorway to assist Second Countryman who supports a helpless Patrick. Patrick is only semi-conscious, with a horrible gash on his forehead. The Countrymen hold him between them. In their free hands they carry message-bags filled with parcels]

First Countryman   We were cycling from the town, Mam. We saw him on the road. He must have fallen from the bike. I said to Jer 'twould be as well to examine him to see who he was, and Jer said to me … *[Voice trails away, seeing Julie upset]*
[Julie immediately guides Patrick with their help to a chair. They seat him]

Julie   Get a towel Sonny and I'll try and bathe this cut.
[Sonny gets towel which he holds to Patrick's forehead.

Julie prepares hot water and a clean cloth to bathe the wound]

First Countryman *[Shyly, apologetically]* We were cycling home from town when we saw him.

Second Countryman *[Ponderous accent]* We saw the bicycle first. There were three of us cycling home. We sent for the doctor by the other fellow. He should be here now.
[Patrick falls forward, in weakness, on the chair. Sonny prevents him from falling. The Countrymen look startled. Julie, who has the water ready by this time, hurries to Patrick's side. The towel is withdrawn. She hands bowl to Sonny dipping cloth in water, surveys wound, bathes]

Julie *[Laving wound]* Will he be here soon?

First Countryman We were an hour bringing him here. *[Indicating Patrick]* The man that went looking for him is bound to find him.

Second Countryman 'Twould take Jimmy half an hour to cycle back to the town. Allow him ten minutes to search. *[Looks towards door]* He should be here now. He knows the doctor's haunts.

First Countryman He should be here by now, all things allowed.

Julie This cut is terrible. *[Laves wound again]*

Sonny *[To Julie]* There's a bottle of iodine in the house somewhere. Would it be any good?

Julie I wouldn't like to use anything on it. I wish the doctor would come. I don't know what to do for him …

Second Countryman He can't be long, whatever is keepin' him. The man we sent is sure to get him.
[At this stage, Patrick recovers consciousness and looks vaguely about him]

Patrick *[Calls faintly, with all his strength]* Eleanor … Eleanor … Eleanor …

Julie Put the bowl on the table. *[To Patrick]* Patrick? … Patrick? … Can you hear me. It's me, Julie. Can you hear me, Patrick? *[To Sonny]* Help me to get him to his bed.

Sonny That's all right now.

First Countryman If he's bad there'll be a priest wanted if he gets worse.

Second Countryman He must have a sight o' whiskey drunk to say he got a fall like that.

First Countryman Come on away out of it. There's enough of 'em here to look after him.
[Enter Mikey again, dazed as before. Looks at newcomers in surprise]

Mikey What's this? What are the two of ye doin' here this hour o' the night?

Second Countryman Your son Patrick had a fall from his bike.

Mikey Bad?

First Countryman The side of his head is all gartered and tore.

Mikey Drunk, I suppose?

Second Countryman There's no doubt he seemed to have a fair share taken.

First Countryman Sure, we all take a sup or two around the Christmas.

Mikey He's always at it! ... I heard a noise, it woke me up ... Is he in his room?

Second Countryman He is. His wife and Sonny are with him ... The Doctor should be here soon.

Mikey What's the doctor for? He'll be all right ... You couldn't kill a drunken man.

First Countryman Well, well be hittin' off.

Mikey *[Change of tone—more pleasure]* Them are great bags of stuff ye have. Presents and whatnots, I suppose, for the Christmas?

Second Countryman The very thing!

Mikey   Would it be any harm now to ask what ye have in them?

[Countrymen exchange looks of surprise]

Mikey   *[Hastily]* I used to be goin' to town one time like yeerselves on Christmas Eve for a few little items when I was younger. I used to bring home big bags of stuff, too, like yeerselves. *[As if remembering]* That was years ago when the boys were young lads and they'd be expectin' little knick-knacks tor their stockings.

First Countryman   *[Puzzled, but eager to please]* Well, there's a duck in my bags and a suit I had repairin' an' a new pair of low shoes an' a bottle o' whiskey … that's all except for a fourpenny bottle o' hair oil.

Mikey   *[To Second Countryman]* What have you in yours?

Second Countryman   *[Hesitantly]* I have a bugle for one of the young lads an' a wax doll for a daughter. There's a pair o' blue bloomers for my missus, a grain o' tea an sugar an' a bit o' mate for the breakfast.

Mikey   *[Very interested]* Mate? … What kind o' mate?

Second Countryman   *[A bit frightened]* Ordinary mate!

Mikey   There's no such thing as ordinary mate. It must be some kind o' mate.

Second Countryman   'Tis just a feed for the breakfast for

myself and the missus an' the young wans. A pound
o' rashers, a pound o' sausages an' a ring o' black puddin'.

Mikey   Black puddin'! ... Did you pay much for it?

Second Countryman   'Twas cheap enough ... only ten-
pence.

Mikey   I'll give you half a crown for it!

Second Countryman   Ah, well, I couldn't sell it...

Mikey   *[Putting hand in pocket]* Five shillin's ...

Second Countryman   Tisn't the money at all, man, but the
missus is very fond of a bit o' black puddin'.

Mikey *[Withdrawing money]* Here ... three half-crowns ...

[Second Countryman nudges First Countryman]

Second Countryman   Three half-crowns ... seven an' six! ...

Mikey   In the palm o' your hand.
*[Mikey puts money in Second Countryman's hand, who
exchanges mystified looks with friend, then gives Mikey
a small paper bag from message bag. Mikey accepts it]*

Mikey   A Happy Christmas now to the two of ye and a safe
journey home.

Countrymen   *[Taking bags and exiting, still puzzled by
Mikey]* Happy Christmas!
[Mikey surveys paper bag for moment, extracts ring of

black pudding. He holds it out to admire it, then takes a large bite and chews with relish. At noise of entry of Julie and Sonny he hastily stuffs pudding into his pocket]

Mikey *[Gulping down pudding]* Well, what way is he?

Julie He seems to be asleep ... Did the two men leave? *[Mikey nods]*

Julie I never thanked them for bringing him home.

Mikey I'll go up and have a look at him ... there's a fellow gone for the doctor.

Sonny We know!
[Exit Mikey]

Julie Sonny! What can be keeping the doctor?

Sonny He'll be all right!
[Julie flops on chair, bends head over table and runs fingers through hair. Sonny barely touching her shoulder, tries to speak but is unable. Julie leans back on chair, wearily. Sonny full of solicitude].

Sonny I'll make a drop of tea for you. You're played out with worry. Tisn't only to-night is all you've gone through since you came. Every single thing was against you from the first day. *[Hurriedly]* I'll make a fresh drop o' *tea* for you now and you'll have a rest then for a while. I'll watch up with him until the doctor comes.

Julie   Sit down, Sonny, please, and talk to me! say anything. Say whatever comes into your head, but, in the name of God, talk to me.
[Worried, Sonny sits on stool]

Sonny   If there was anything in the world that I could do, I'd do it.

Julie   *[Reaches out hand and covers one of Sonny's]* You're the only friend I have here, and you've been good and kind to me from the start. You took me the way you found me and I appreciate your friendship.

Sonny   *[Near to tears]* I'd give all I have in the world to see the worry goin' from your face.

Julie   I'm not worth so much kindness from anybody.

Sonny   'Tis a hard Christmas for you.

Julie   I've seen some hard Christmas mornings before this, Sonny. *[Looks anxiously towards Patrick's room]*

Sonny   *[Embarrassedly]* 'Twas good you understood about the woman at the 'bus. No one else would. I'm a different man since I got it out of my mind. Patrick will be all right, please God! The bleedin' is stopped an' that's surely a good sign. *[Forced cheerfulness]* 'Twill make a bright Christmas mornin' yet, please God.
[Enter Connie, takes a basin and washes hands]

Connie   *[Triumph]* The red cow calved ... a fine heifer calf

... without a bit of trouble ... where's my father?

Sonny *[Bitterly]* In the room above. Patrick had a fall. We're waitin' for the doctor now.

Connie What did you expect, the way he was drinking?

Sonny Shut up, and leave us alone!
[Connie stands back astonished]

Connie You're telling me to shut up ... You know what I'm going to do to you? I'm going to kick your pants so hard that the sight of a chair will make you sick.
[Kicks stool from under Sonny]

Julie Leave him alone!

Connie *[Mock wonder]* What's goin' on in here? *[Surveys the two of them leeringly]* Don't tell me you've fallen for her Sonny; *[Laughs]* Oh, you poor stupid bastard.
[Enter Mikey, shocked, in a state of panic]

Mikey *[To Julie]* Julie, Sonny, Quick! ... Go up to him! He's fighting for breath.
[Julie rises and hurries to room]

Mikey *[In awe, to Sonny]* He gave a small cry an' then a few terrible heaves. He's dead, I think!

Connie *[Seeing his father's sorrow]* I'm sorry, Dad ...

Mikey *[Vacantly, sorrowfully]* Patrick ... Patrick ..

Connie *[Thinking to cheer up his father]* The ... the red cow is calved. Dad ... a heifer calf with a white ring on her neck.

[*Mikey looks at him with disbelief for a moment, then with utter contempt, then with fury*]

Mikey [*With restrained fury*] Will you see your brother damned forever in Hell? [*Hoarsely*] Will you? [*Louder*]: Start runnin' now across the bog with all the strength of your four bones. [*Loudly in disgust*] Run till your cowardly heart stops an' the shame is driven out of you. Run, you Godless whelp, an' find a priest from the House o' Christ for my son.

[*Connie retreats frightened. He exits as Mikey raises clenched fist over his head to strike him and looks wildly around for a weapon and impotently flings the contents of his pockets after Connie, then turns brokenly*]

Mikey Patrick ... Patrick ...

[*Enter Sonny and Julie*]

Mikey We'll have to make the room ready for the priest; we'll go up together now and we'll kneel and say the rosary for the soul of my dead son.

Julie And my dead husband.

[*Mikey turns Julie back towards stairs. She collapses on floor*]

ACT THREE

SCENE ONE

Action takes place as before. The time is a month later. It is the afternoon. Julie stands over table, dressed sombrely. She is ironing clothes with a large flat-iron. Sonny sits at the fire. Julie is not what she was since Patrick's death, looks at her searchingly. That is evident from her dress and carriage. Sonny

Sonny   Maybe 'tis wrong for me to say it, Julie ... but 'tis a month now since the funeral ... and ... well you should ... you should be comin' outa yourself. *[Depressed, unaware of his words, Julie irons away. Sonny rises, but doesn't move otherwise]*

Sonny   *[Hesitant, unsure of himself]* Patrick is dead, Julie Nothin' will bring him back.

Julie   He didn't love me, Sonny! He never loved me!

Sonny   You shouldn't let yourself be thinkin' about that side of it at all.

Julie   But he didn't, Sonny. That other woman was all he thought about.

Sonny   Sure, what about it if he called her name a few times when he was in drink.

Julie   I'll have to leave here soon, that's for certain and sure.

Sonny   *[Dejectedly]* When?

Julie   I can't go for some time.

Sonny   Is your mind made up to go?

Julie   *[Restraining tears]*: I shouldn't stay here. But when I think about it I find I have no place else to go.

Sonny   *[Eagerly, Hopefully]* Stay here! What's to hunt you? Things will be quiet here, and we'll see after you well.

Julie   I don't want to go back but I must. I must get out of this house. If you could only understand, Sonny. I must get out and get away.
[Dejectedly Sonny crosses kitchen and opens kitchen door. Looking out]

Sonny   I think I'll go away again myself. When you came here it was like the light o' sunshine proddin' its way through the branches of a thorny tree. When you go I'll throw my shoes away from me again. I'll lie down in the rain in the wet heath outside my door and I'll think with all my heart of the time you were here. I'll think of the first time you came to the house with Patrick. *[Turns and looks at her]* I'll be always sayin' to myself: " Where's Julie now? " " Where is the bright girl that came here and gone an' who'll see that nothin' will come to harm her?"
[Enter Connie. He looks at both with sly humour]

Connie *[To Julie]* How do you stand him all day with his calf's eyes and his tongue hanging out?

Julie Why don't you pick on somebody who's not afraid of you?

Sonny *[Rises]* I'll get the milk for the tea.
[Sonny moves towards door. Connie pretends to be about to assault him. Sonny backs, Connie laughs and turns his attention to Julie. Exit Sonny]

Connie I'll be going to town to-night. Would you like to come in—or take in a picture? Or if you'd rather, a drink?

Julie No, thank you!

Connie Is there anything you want? I could bring it to you.

Julie *[Coldly]* You might bring some flour. There's none in the house. And there's tea and sugar and soap. Sonny has the list of messages. He'll give it to you.

Connie Oh, I don't mean that! What I mean is, is there anything you want for yourself ...

Julie I want nothing from you ...

Connie Nothing! ... You don't mean that?

Julie Do you need any further proof?

Connie I'm only trying to help.

Julie Haven't you got work to do? What about the dykes

you were supposed to do?

Connie   *[Proudly]* All done !

Julie   And the hedges?

Connie   I'm strong! *[Flexes himself]* I finished them … *[With an innocent air]* What are your plans?

Connie   Yes, what are you going to do now?

Julie   What are you talking about?

Connie   When are you going? Is that simple enough?

Julie   What's it to you if I go or stay?

Connie   If you're staying here, we can't go on like this.

Julie   Like what?

Connie   Well, you can't go on treating me as if I were an animal.

Julie   Why not?

Connie   You know how I feel for you … God dammit, you must know I'm not a bloody dog that will follow you around. I'm a man!

Julie   You don't ever give up, do you!

Connie   Why do you dislike me so much?

Julie   *[Bitterly]* Oh, I don't dislike you! I just hate the sight of you! That's all!

Connie *[Slyly, undaunted]* I'll wear you down; I'll keep telling you every day how much I love you, and then, one day you'll say to yourself; " Maybe he means it! He's not so bad after all! "

Julie *[Laughs scornfully]* I honestly believe you don't know what you want. You're insecure and lonely and a terrible coward at heart. That makes you a bully. You don't want me. You don't love me, because you don't love anything.

Connie I never think of anything but you. I think about your hair, eyes and smile, and ... and your body. You have a really fine body.

Julie *[Sharply]* Stop it!

Connie But I do think about you.

Julie You really sound convincing. *[Connie is about to rage but changes his mind]* But you know what I am, don't you? You should know better than to try that with me.

Connie *[Slyly]* I bet if I had you in my arms; you'd change your mind. You're a woman, aren't you ... not a bloody block of wood.

Julie All right then, try. What's wrong? This was what you wanted, isn't it?
[Connie attempts to put a hand on her. Julie seizes the flat-iron suddenly and presses it against his hand. He

jumps backward suddenly, clutching his hand in pain. Julie holds the iron poised]

Connie You bitch, I'll get even with you, you dirty Piccadilly prostitute. Patrick may have stood for it, but by Christ I won't. I'll trample you back into the dirt you came out of.
[Julie has gone up the stairs. Connie turns and finds Mikey in the doorway]

Mikey What's all the shouting about? I was watering the calves in the byre and I thought you must be murdering someone.

Connie She's bloody lucky, Da that I didn't kill her … Look what she's done to me!

Mikey Take it easy now, Connie, 'twas only an accident.

Connie 'Twas no accident Da. She meant it all right, the bloody bitch.

Mikey That's no way to talk of Julie. She's a fine woman Connie and she's made a great change in this house. I won't have you say one word against her. She's like a daughter to me now.

Connie God forbid!

Mikey What do you mean?

Connie I hate to say this, on account of Patrick, but I think you should know, Da.

Mikey   Know what?

Connie   I think you should know the kind of a woman she is.

Mikey   What are you trying to tell me … Come on, out with it man.

Connie   All right—I'll tell you so. She's nothing but a bloody prostitute.

Mikey   How could that be true? She married Patrick … didn't she?

Connie   And look how he ended up. I suppose it was when he found out about her that he started hitting the bottle. You know he never drank before he left here.

Mikey   That's true—but no, no, no—Julie's not like that. She's too good in herself to be one o' them. No, Connie … there's something wrong somewhere. Who told you this?

Connie   'Twas no one but herself, Da, and I'll tell you how it happened. I came in to get a packet o' cigarettes and she was standing there ironing. I brushed past her and "Where are you going? " says she; " to my bedroom " says I. Then she came over and stood real close to me. "You could have me beside you any night " says she. I didn't know what to say or do — I just stood there looking at her. And then she laughed into my face.

Mikey   My God!

Connie   I told her pack her bags and get out, Da, and then I told her I was going out to tell you. That's when she made for me with the red-hot iron.

Mikey   You've said enough, son. Leave me 'till I talk with her.

Connie   Have no talk at all with her, Da. Just let her get to Hell out of here. She's not good for us. I've done without a woman in this house for years.

Mikey   Yes, Connie ... I've done without a woman for years. Can still do without one. Go out Connie and leave me to deal with this. *[Calling]* Julie! Julie! *[Exit Connie ... Julie comes down the stairs with her bags]*

Mikey   Is it true what he told me? His arm is burned outside an he's after swearin' on his soul an conscience that it's true.

Julie   What did he tell you?

Mikey   He told me you were one of them women!

Julie   He told you the truth. I was. But I'm not any more. Did he tell you that? Did he tell you why I burned him, or did he just tell you what I was and no more!

Mikey   *[Flabbergasted, but not terribly angry]* 'Tis true so, I don't know what to say to you. I don't know.

[*Puzzled and confused*] Why, in the name of God, did you come here to us if you're a woman like that? What will the people say? What will the priest say?

Julie The priest won't say anything. He'll be the first to forgive.

Mikey No—no! I can't have it! You'll have to go! ... I've nothing against you—take care o' that, but I don't want you staying on here.

Julie I haven't any place to go ... I'm having a baby!

Mikey [*Fearful*] ... A baby!

Julie Let me stay a short while until I make arrangements.

Mikey [*Panic*] No—no! I couldn't! There's places in the city. They'll look after you.

Julie Only for a few weeks, until I find a place.

Mikey [*Vehemently*] No! ... No! ... Never! Why do you think I went for all these years without a servant girl in the house. Why is it I never had a woman in to cook and give this place the appearance of a home? I wouldn't dare trust myself an' that's why I've been a sane man all these years, because I'm afraid of myself.

Julie But I promise I won't come in the way. I promise I'll do anything until after the baby.

113

Mikey   *[Suddenly changes tone and stance]*: Anything? …

Julie   I didn't mean that…

Mikey   *[Slurred, thickly]* 'Tis years …
[Julie tries to draw away]

Julie   Oh, my God!

Mikey   *[Look at her foolishly]* I never met one o' your equals.
I heard tell o' ye often from the lads comin' across
the water but I never seen one till now … 'Tis years
and years …
[Julie moves to stairs quickly, violently]

Julie   Get out … out … out! Are you all rotten here?
[Runs up stairs]
[Mikey backs horrified, realising what he has done]

Mikey   I'm sorry … I'm sorry … I'm mortally sorry. *[Low
tone of menace]*… 'Twould never have happened if I
wasn't told … Now I'm man no more, an' 'twas that
cur that told me … *[Gentler mood]* Forgive me, Julie,
for a thing I never did in my life … Forgive me,
girl … *[Enter Sonny with a gallon of milk. Mikey sees
him and brushes past him hurriedly without looking
his way. Sonny pours milk in churn and puts can on
dresser]*

Sonny   What did he say to you?

Julie   Nothing … It's not important … He didn't mean
what he said. *[She looks directly at Sonny]*

Julie   Why are you looking at me like that?
               [Sonny looks very embarrassed]

Julie   He told you? *[Sonny nods—Julie hangs head]*
               [Sonny too ashamed of feelings to reply]

Sonny   He told me.

Julie   Say what you think because what you think is what
               matters.

Sonny   What they said is nothin' to me. What I say is, if
               they're all like you—them people they mentioned
               you were one of—there should be no condemnin' of
               'em. 'Tis a shame the way they put names on people.
               *[Julie turns away, then turns suddenly again, near to
               tears, sits near table]*

Julie   It isn't quite true, Sonny. Not all of it. *[Tears]* All I
               wanted was someone to take care of me; someone
               to love me.

Sonny   God help us, you had a worse time of it than myself
               an' there was I complainin' to you an' tellin' you
               about my hurt an' you listenin' to me an' consolin me
               with never a word about your own troubles. God
               help us— what did I suffer only a few dotin' oul'
               dreams that were for children.

Julie   *[Smiles]* I should have known my Sonny.

Sonny   They said you'd be leavin' soon. They're in league
               against you. Where'll you go? How'll you manage at

all when you'll be alone?

Julie   I don't know yet. I'll find somewhere.

Sonny   I know a fellow that'll buy my heifers on the spot. I can give you a good bit o' money goin'.

Julie   No ... You'll want it for yourself. I couldn't take it, Sonny.

Sonny   They told me you were goin' to have a child!

Julie   That's true, too.

Sonny   Sure, how would you manage that and support yourself as well.

Julie   I'll find a place.

Sonny   When will you be goin'?

Julie   I don't know yet. I'll have to think about it. I'll try to get away tomorrow if I can.

Sonny   I can get the money tonight. You'll have to take it. I won't hear of you sayin' no again ...

Julie   'Twould only be a loan.

Sonny   Oh, good God, no! I want you to keep it an' don't think of it. Sure, what do I want it for? I never go anywhere anyway, I have my house and farm on the mountain. I'll have to go back there now. *[Sad note]* 'Twill be better than here. They leave me alone there.

116

Julie   It must be terribly lonely, living all alone on a mountain.

Sonny   No, it's not lonely. It's healthy an' clean an' the only people you meet are the few odd mountainy people an' they're the friendliest people at all when you know them. They'd never let a man starve up there anyway, and they have little to do with the people down here. And 'tis like a garden up there in the summer. Down below in the bogs you can see the white canavaun covering the land an' all around the heather is bloomin' an' there's a smell o' the wild mountain meadows an' there's the maddest an' gayest larks on the face o' creation up there.

Julie   It's like heaven.

Sonny   [*Warming to his theme*] 'Tis all that! Away from you there's the miles an' miles o' country an' you can see four counties an' the sight o' the Shannon River being gathered up by the sea. Me an' Mikey were born up there. My father bought this place for Mikey but he left the highest house to me.

Julie   I can almost imagine it.

Sonny   You'll hear the scholars an' they singin' the Irish songs an' they passin' over the mountain to school. You'll see the hares dancin' if you lie still in the high heather an' the little strames would be callin 'to you all the time. Then, in the winter, there's the snow

117

an' it's beautiful, too. That's the time for big fires an' maybe ramblin' to visit a neighbour. There's great nights there around the Christmas ... melodeons an' fiddles an' drums an' dancin' in the kitchens 'till cockcrow.

Julie   You love the mountain, Sonny, don't you?

Sonny   No place better, but I got lonesome an' strange, an' then Mikey was all alone down here, so down I came an' I stayed for a while an' then you came an' you made a man o' me.

Julie   I'll miss you, Sonny!

Sonny   An' I'll miss you.
[Julie turns her head from his gaze, with some embarrassment]

Sonny   *[Turning away]* I have to say this thing to you. Don't go away at all, Julie. Stay here. Whatever you do, don't go!

Julie   No ... no ... Sonny, I can't ... I can't stay here.

Sonny   *[Pleads]* Listen, so. Listen, Julie. Would you come with me an' put my life together. Would you come an' I'd give you peace an ease an provide for yourself an' the little creature we don't see. I don't know what love is, Julie, or the meanin' of it or I don't know what way is the right way to talk to a woman at all. All I know is that if you go away from here

an' if I never see you again, I'll sit above in the bare mountain without bite or sup, or without thought of any kind. I know it, Julie! When you're gone I'll lie down in the wind an' snow an' leave death come to me an' death will be an ease to me an' a blessin' ...
[Julie notices him patiently, but with pity]

Julie   No, Sonny, you don't know what you're saying.

Sonny   You're the only life or happiness I've ever known.

Julie   No ... no ... I'm not what you think!

Sonny   *[Horrified]* Don't say it for you're an angel, an' for a fellow like me to know you even, is a blessing.. I'd work from the first light to the last light for you.. Come away with me an' I'll ask no love or comfort from you or no sign of love only let me look after you, an' let the long years heal your hurt.

Julie   You mustn't say any more, Sonny. I'm not worth thinking about.
[Enter Connie as Julie exits to her room]

Connie   What goes on between you and that one? You know what she is, don't you?

Sonny   I do! She's a saint!

Connie   Remind me to make a novena to her.

Sonny   You'll never get Julie to eat out of your hand, anyone but her!

[Enter Mikey]

Mikey   Go outside, Sonny.

Sonny   What is it Mikey, what's wrong?

Mikey   Leave us, Sonny.
[Exit Sonny]

Mikey   *[To Connie]* 'Twas you, 'twas you put it into my head, when you told me what she was.

Connie   What do you mean?

Mikey   No woman ever accused me of provoking or disturbing her, but to go approaching my dead son's widow, to go near Julie, to try to lay hands on her; you caused it, you God damned curse that caused all my troubles since the day you were born!

Connie   *[Backing away]* That wasn't why I told you. 'Twas to get the farm I told you.

Mikey   Amn't I the same as any other man? Do you think I've forgotten what a woman is?

Connie   *[Backs away further]* I'm sorry, Dad.

Mikey   You're sorry; you're always sorry, you rotting corpse. *[Clutches Connie]* You think there is a way out for you, but not this time! Let God judge me for what I'm going to do, for this time I'll beat you until your blood flows from you, and I'll whip you from my door.

[*As Connie is cowering, half kneeling in Mikey's grip, Sheila enters*]

Sheila   Connie, Connie, Connie!
[*Connie rises as Mikey stops Sheila*]

Mikey   What has you here?

Sheila   They're coming for him, my father, and my brothers
and a gang with them. They tried to lock me in, but
I ran away. You must go Connie, you must run.

Mikey   You must not run. [*Pushing Connie to floor*] You'll
not run from me when I've done with you. You can
take your riven bones and beat them on the flag-
stones of Hell. [*Turns to look at Sheila*]

Sheila   Why do you hate him when he needs you so much?
… He needs you and no more. In your heart you
know that he's your son, but you won't admit that
you love him.

Mikey   Go away; leave me be. [*Looks at Connie*]

Sheila   You turn him from you when he needs *you* most,
You are the only one he has when every man's blood
is turned against him. He needs you, and no one
can help him now but his own father. What sort
of a father are you that you wont protect your own
son?
[*During this speech Mikey has crossed slowly to Connie*]

Mikey   There will no man interfere with my son. I sired him. I don't give a hells curse what he did, and I'll answer to any man for my son. *[Raises Connie to his feet]*

[Angry shouts outside. Sheila goes to window]

Sheila   They're here!

Mikey   I don't care about other men's sons, but this one is mine, and I know his weaknesses because they are my weaknesses, and I know his passion because I was the seed of his passion.

Voices Off   Come out Connie Bannon, come out you

Mikey   *[Crossing to door]* What hell's bastard dared say a word of my son? What mange-ridden son of a bitch would dare tamper with us? What man would risk his like to come between me and my true-blooded son?

Voices Off   Send him out to us. Send him out to his just deserts. There's no ill will to you, Mikey Bannon.

Mikey   Ill will to my son is ill will to me. Defend your family Ned Molony, and I'll defend mine.

Voices Off There's twenty of us here; if you won't send him, we'll come and take him, and if you're harmed the blood is not on us. I'll give you a count of ten to send the coward out.

[The count starts, interrupted by menacing roars of crowd]

Connie *[As count reaches ten and is followed by roar]* Shut up—what I've done I'll answer for, but twenty of you won't come for me and call me a coward. I'll go to you and face you on my own.

Mikey We'll go together, son!
[Connie has noticed the billhook and grabs it on way out just behind Mikey; ignoring Sheila who tries to stop him. Julie goes to the door and Sheila to the window. There is absolute silence outside]

Sheila They're walking straight up to the crowd, we must stop them. *[She dashes to door, but is stopped by Julie]*

Julie Stay where you are; no one must stop them now.

Sheila They're facing each other; my father and twenty men on one side, Connie and Mikey on the other.

Julie There's Sonny, he's trying to come between them.

Sonny *[Off]* Men, men, in God's Name, men, let there be peace between you.

Connie *[Off]* Keep back Sonny, it's me they want. All right, I'm coming.
[A pause, then a roar from the crowd]

Sheila Connie has run straight from them; they're all on him.

Julie It's all stopped. Sonny is coming this way and

they're all turning away. Mikey is kneeling on the ground holding Connie.

Sheila   They've killed him. *[Shouts as she exits by door]* Connie, Connie, Connie!
[Enter Sonny]

Sonny   It was all so quick. I tried to stop them—they might have stopped, for they didn't come to kill Connie, only to pay him out for what he'd done to Sheila. But it was so quick. Connie threw me to one side, and ran at them before Mikey could stop him. I think maybe he had it planned so that me and Mikey would come to no hurt. There was nothing we could do. They were all on him roaring. In all me life I never knew that death could come so quick.
[Enter Mikey]

Mikey   *[To Julie]* Both dead, and you the cause.

Sonny   There's been enough of bitterness, Mikey.

Mikey   There's nothing but bitterness when there's sin in people's hearts. *[Sinks into armchair]* Go now, leave me in my house alone, till the agony runs from me in God's own healing time.
[Julie to the stairs for suitcase. Sonny crosses to the foot of the stair as Julie comes down]

Sonny   *[Full of hurt]* Where are you going? What will you do?

Julie   Where am I going …? *[Full of tenderness]* I'm going to the highest house on the mountain. Where else would I be going but with you …

Sonny   Oh, my God! … *[Touches her hand]* … Oh, my God! … what right have I …? Oh, my God, Julie, never in my life did I dream that such a joy would come to me …

Julie   I'll go to any part of the world with you Sonny. I'd share mattress, field or form with you because we have a chance with each other. Together we have a chance. Get your things now and we'll be going.

Sonny   I have no things. *[Proudly]* My things are all above on the mountain.
[Julie gives bag to Sonny and they go. After a pause Sheila enters to Mikey who has remained motionless]
[Time lag]

Sheila   The priest is coming and the neighbours will be bringing Connie soon to the house. *[Sits on stool]*

Mikey   I knelt awhile over my dead son. I felt the damp of the mountain in my knees and I thought to myself 'tis creeping now over the body of Connie like the damp of the grave is creeping over Patrick. This is a house of the dead, for a man's home dies when his blood and his breed will come through his door no more. I'll not cry like you cried, Sheila and you running across the mountain for the priest, a woman

125

will cry for death, but a man is beyond tears in the face of his Almighty God. I'll sit awhile and wait for the neighbours to bring his body home. I'll tell them, at the wake, how he died in the semblance of a man. Connie took his last chance to show that my seed may fail but will not rot and it's little enough chance any of us had to show that God's created men are greater than the beasts that tramp the fields.

ABOUT THE AUTHOR

John B. Keane, one of Ireland's most prolific and respected literary figures, died on 30 May 2002 at the age of 73, after a long and difficult battle with cancer. He was born in 1928 in Listowel, County Kerry and it was here that he spent his literary career, running a pub which provided him with inspiration for his characters and ideas.

His first play, *Sive*, was presented by the Listowel Drama Group and won the All-Ireland Drama Festival in 1959. It was followed by another success, *Sharon's Grave*, in 1960. *The Field* [1965] and *Big Maggie* [1969], are widely regarded as classics of the modern Irish stage and jewels in a crown which includes such popular hits as *Many Young Men of Twenty*, *The Man from Clare*, *Moll*, *The Chastitute* and *The Year of the Hiker*. His large canon of plays has been seen abroad in cities as far afield as Moscow and Los Angeles. *Big Maggie* ran on Broadway for over two months in 1982 and *The Field* was adapted into an Oscar-winning Hollywood film, starring Brenda Fricker and Richard Harris, in 1991.

But it was not just in his plays that John B. Keane managed to portray all aspects of humanity with both wit and truth. He also wrote many fine novels, including *The Contractors*, *A High Meadow* and *Durango*. *Durango* was adapted for the big screen, starring Brenda Fricker and Patrick Bergin. A writer of essays, short stories and letters, his humorous words live on in *Celebrated Letters of John B. Keane*, *More Celebrated Letters*, *The Best of John B. Keane* and *The Short Stories of John B. Keane*. In 1987 John B. Keane received a special award for his enduring place in Irish life and letters from the *Sunday Independent/Irish Life*. In that year he also won a *Sunday Tribune* Arts Award and in 1988 he was chosen as the recipient of the Irish-American Fund Award for Literature. In 1999 he was presented with a Gradam medal, the Abbey Theatre's highest award.

He was a member of Aosdana and the recipient of honorary doctorates from Trinity College, Dublin, Limerick University and Marymount College, New York. John B. Keane remains one of Mercier's best-loved and best-selling authors.